Declare the following regarding Robin Hood:

"He is now legally, and not simply in effect, an outlaw," Geoffrey said. *"Any man who finds him can kill him with impunity. The law offers him nothing, not mercy, not recognition of name or status, nor does it see him as a child under the roof of the king's power. It is as if he were not born."*

Henry bowed. It was no easy thing, condemning a man. Henry marched into the darkness that surrounded them, a man carrying out a death warrant.

Geoffrey sat heavily. The command had taken the last fire out of him. "Don't worry for even a moment, Baldwin. I will net this man, and every man with him, because to catch one fly is nothing. I will catch them all. With a trick."

"In a Dark Wood is a stunning tour de force, beautifully written, in which Michael Cadnum turns the legend of Robin Hood inside out. Cadnum's shimmering prose is poetry with muscle, capturing both the beauty and brutality of life in Nottinghamshire. *In a Dark Wood* may well become that rare thing—an enduring piece of literature."

—Robert Cormier, author of *The Chocolate War*

OTHER PUFFIN BOOKS YOU MAY ENJOY

In a Dark Wood

Michael Cadnum

PUFFIN BOOKS

PUFFIN BOOKS
Published by the Penguin Group
Penguin Putnam Books for Young Readers,
345 Hudson Street, New York, New York 10014, U.S.A.
Penguin Books Ltd, 27 Wrights Lane, London W8 5TZ, England
Penguin Books Australia Ltd, Ringwood, Victoria, Australia
Penguin Books Canada Ltd, 10 Alcorn Avenue, Toronto, Ontario, Canada M4V 3B2
Penguin Books (N.Z.) Ltd, 182-190 Wairau Road, Auckland 10, New Zealand

Penguin Books Ltd, Registered Offices: Harmondsworth, Middlesex, England

First published in the United States of America by Orchard Books, 1998
Published by Puffin Books,
a member of Penguin Putnam Books for Young Readers, 1999

1 3 5 7 9 10 8 6 4 2

LIBRARY OF CONGRESS CATALOGING-IN-PUBLICATION DATA
Cadnum, Michael.
In a dark wood / Michael Cadnum.
p. cm.
Summary: On orders from the King, the Sheriff of Nottingham seeks to capture
the outlaw Robin Hood, but he finds him to be a tricky and elusive foe.
ISBN 0-14-130638-6 (pbk.)
1. Sheriff of Nottingham (Legendary character) Juvenile fiction. 2. Robin Hood
(Legendary character) Juvenile fiction. 3. Great Britain—History—Richard I,
1189–1199 Juvenile fiction.
[1. Sheriff of Nottingham (Legendary character) Fiction. 2. Robin Hood
(Legendary character) Fiction. 3. Great Britain—History—Richard I, 1189–1199
Fiction. 4. Robbers and outlaws Fiction.]
I. Title.
PZ7.C11724In 1999 [Fic]—dc21 99-21408 CIP

Printed in the United States of America

The bay
the color of the bay
in the air

Midway in our life's journey
I found myself in a dark wood,
the right road lost.

—DANTE,
The Inferno

1

The forest was quiet. Everything that was about to happen was far away, through the trees.

Geoffrey stood still, staring straight ahead, although he could see nothing but trembling patches of sunlight on the fallen leaves. A forest was like night. It was a different world, and everything a man was afraid of lived there, afraid of nothing.

The boar spear was a long, heavy weapon, and this particular spear had never been used before. Its head was slender and very sharp, and the cross-piece midway down the shaft was gleaming black. Geoffrey found a new grip on the spear, the iron cold where he had not touched it, and the horns of the beaters, and their cries, filtered through the trees, bright curls of sounds, like shavings on a goldsmith's bench.

Between them and where he stood was the most dangerous kind of beast. It could feel no pain. Its eyes were fire pricks. It weighed more than three men.

And it was coming his way. Hugh, the squire beside him, shivered. His crossbow was loaded and cocked and aimed at the empty place before them. The youth's lips were tight, and he would not meet Geoffrey's eye. Geoffrey tried to utter reassurance. His tongue was so dry he merely croaked, and he pretended to cough.

No hounds today, he had laughed. No, let the dogs stay penned. Today he would take one man to man. Approving laughter. The chief huntsman leaping into his saddle with a fart. An excellent day for it. Geoffrey would provide them with enough proof of his own courage to last a year. Unless the spear slipped, as he had seen it slip in the past.

Horns on three sides now. Birds struggled through the air, magpies flashing black and crisp white, and a crow like fresh iron falling from one branch to another, not even calling, working itself north.

He would not have said this to Hugh, but he could admit it to himself. Sometimes, in the full feast of a day's events, he experienced a twinge of cowardice.

The forest was too quiet. Even the sparrows hushed. A tree ahead of them shook itself, like a man just come in from great cold. A bush swayed, and a twig snapped, one of those common twigs, bare of leaves, that crook like a finger of dancing death as he leaps into the road before the traveler.

Geoffrey wanted to protect Hugh from any harm. At times it was hard to know what words to use with the fourteen-year-old. Sometimes Geoffrey felt that Hugh was like a son, but he couldn't think of a way to put the feeling into speech.

The hunt fences, hidden barriers in the woods, would prevent the beast from any course but this. Geoffrey gazed upwards at the cross-span, then planted the spear at his instep and placed his left foot forwards. He crouched, his fingers finding dry places on the cold iron. A horn again, a smear of sound, like snot on wool, and then it happened.

Too quickly. Two huge nostrils, black and snorting. Eyes too small—how could they be so small? One tusk curved out more than the other, like moustaches knocked awry. A leap, and four legs that were too slender for such a huge head were in midair, the small eyes growing not larger as they approached, but smaller, recognizing who he was and what was wrong with him.

The animal didn't even see the spear. It met him between the tusks, and the jolt bent the iron shaft just perceptibly, and then the spear straightened as the boar fought his way up the shaft, snarling like a demon struggling against flood. A spume of pink flung itself from one nostril, and then both nostrils closed like eyes and opened again as the monster reached the cross-beam and wrenched the spear out of Geoffrey's hands.

Geoffrey fought for the iron, but the spear knocked him off his feet, whipped and knocked him again, and this time he held it, but too close to the cross-bar, and the bristles seared him, and twin spouts of pink foam blinded him as he struggled to have enough breath to call, "Now!"

The crossbow quarrel kicked the beast off its front

3

feet, and the spear shaft wrestled with Geoffrey as he found a span that was not hot with blood and fat and stood to put his weight into it. At that moment, as he stood, too weak to do more than he was doing, hanging on to a length of iron like a drowning man to a rope, the two tiny eyes of the monster pulled themselves back, leaving empty black holes, and the creature was dead.

The dead beast was on Geoffrey in an instant, the hard wires of its belly stinging his cheek, just as the chief huntsman called, "Hoy!" A hard foreleg crushed out all the air he had ever breathed, hooves grinding him into the earth. The monster ran the butt of the spear into a tree and fell sideways, shuddering.

The chief huntsman held his sword into the sunlight that streaked down through the trees and knelt to his work. "He's dead enough now," he said, pronouncing the word "deed," the way everyone here pronounced it, in the dialect that seemed invented to be used by hunters, crisp, with gutturals and short, rough words, like the crackling of leaves.

The head stared from its stake and then looked up at the sky as men forced the stake into the ground. The tusks were whiter now, and the eyes had regained their glint. Death was only a pause.

"Good work, my lord," said the chief huntsman, and Geoffrey knew Ralf well enough to know that compliments were not wasted. Ralf split the carcass along the spine and emptied the gray bowels on the mulch. "Pity to waste the parts the hounds love best," said the huntsman, thinking always of his dogs or his horses, of any animal at all, rather than waste thoughts on humans.

4

"Mixed with bread, as always, they love it. Makes them feel God's strength." He would have built a fire and braised the innards on coals to the hounds' great pleasure.

For the men it was a rich moment. Their chief, their master, their employer and purpose, had done well. He had shown strength, and now a rich bounty was theirs. Pride, and a feast. They were true men to serve as the arms and legs of such a man. They, who were at home here in the night-dark woods, hoisted the halves of the carcass and carried it quickly in the wake of the head.

2

ugh followed the sheriff on a palfrey, a horse bred for ease and beauty, not for war. I didn't disgrace myself, thought Hugh. The forest shadows, the coughing boar, the flying blood—it was the stuff of a nightmare. But the sheriff did not notice how I trembled.

Hugh lived for a word of praise from the sheriff, and while such praise was very rare, Hugh believed that if he learned to be strong, someday he would be the sheriff's sword arm, a better fighter than Henry. And someday— Hugh let himself think such a high thought—someday he would sit at the sheriff's side at the council table and the sheriff would turn to him and say, "Hugh, what do you think?" Or, "Hugh, what shall we do?"

The boar's head gaped across the field, rising and falling with the steady pace of the huntsmen. It turned on its stick to survey the field and turned back again to look up the road towards Geoffrey.

"A fine sight," breathed Hugh.

And then he silenced himself. It was not likely that the sheriff was interested in Hugh's opinion or how proud Hugh himself felt at being present at such a hunt.

Why, thought Geoffrey, can't I tell Hugh how bravely he behaved, despite his obvious—understandable—alarm at the sight of the boar? Some awkwardness, a clumsy silence, fell upon the sheriff whenever he began to express affection.

The field was cluttered with birds. A scarecrow on a stick held a bow and arrow, like half a man miraculously endowed with the power to fight or at least kill magpies. A horse dragged a wooden frame weighted with a stone, the comblike teeth of the frame breaking the earth into perfect lines. The borders of the field were ragged with green. Trees with thick, stumpy trunks raised branches in shocks. A peasant with a white cap stretched down over his ears sat astride the horse, flourishing a small whip. The horse was stocky and shaggy. It shat, and the teeth of the wooden frame combed the golden manure into the field.

Geoffrey knew that at night, in May, when the full moon rose like a petal on black water, such a man led his wife into the plow-ridged fields. He laid her down on the dirt, lifted her smock, and grunted like a bull under the glittering sky so that the earth would rouse from her sleep and remember her duty. The farm folk often recalled such ancient rites.

"Lady Eleanor goes fowling this afternoon," said Hugh.

This was not conversation. This was a report, and Geoffrey turned in his saddle to see a gown cascade from the side of a horse and wings flutter from wrists.

Geoffrey looked back towards the forest. The grinning head approached, bobbing at the end of its stick.

He wrapped the reins round his hand so tightly it hurt, and ground his teeth. He was trapped between the devil's face in one direction and the devil's work in the other. He glanced at Hugh and forced a smile. "It will be our good fortune to wish them success."

"It's already proven a perfect afternoon for the kill," said Hugh, and if he understood anything at all, his expression did not show it.

"Only the stars are perfect," said Geoffrey.

A quick contradiction was the signal that his lord wanted silence, and Hugh looked away, studying a flock of blackbirds.

The falconer dragged a long stick, a graceful arc of wood, and two falcons gripped his gloved hand. He wore one red stocking and one black, and his sleeves were rolled up, baring two brown arms. Two small wire-haired dogs danced and sniffed the dirt. Lady Eleanor's reins were decorated with red fringes and gleaming buttons, and the horse fought the bit with its tongue.

She rode side-saddle, her head protected by a white wimple, its shadow falling over her shoulders. Her black dress flowed with the prancing of the horse, but her red silk sleeves were tight. Her gloves were tight, too, so close-fitting she had struggled to force each finger into each even more slender sheath. A falcon turned its head at the sound of her voice, the gray cloth of its hood like the cowl of a monk.

"I knew we'd see you," she said.

"I thought you were sick," said Geoffrey with a smile.

"It passed," said his wife, the drape of her wimple hiding her face as she said to one of the dogs, "and I decided to amuse myself."

Geoffrey balled his fist so tightly a knuckle cracked. "I'm glad you're feeling better," he said, and pulled his horse into the ragged border of the field.

At that moment the huntsmen arrived with the huge head dripping black, its fine black eye pricks taking him in and knowing him, comprehending him entirely and not with contempt. With understanding, fellowship even.

"It was quick work," said Hugh, eager to tell it. Geoffrey flushed with pleasure at the tale of a flying beast, a spear in a sure hand, dust, blood. All in a young man's chatter.

"I know all about what goes on in the forest," she said, and long after her skitterish horse and nervous dogs had slipped by the carcass, her words hung round him like a necklace of thorns.

3

The clop of hoof among walls soothed Geoffrey. Straw on stone. Baskets of green apples. Barrels of ale lifted into carts by groaning men. And everywhere a glance of respect.

This was where he belonged, in the shadow of walls. The drawbridge resounded beneath him, and the stone-paved courtyard was so pleasing to him that he leaped unaided and strode across it to the chapel, where he gave thanks for his courage and for his fortitude in the face of his wife. His wife—that thought snapped his gratitude for a moment, and he turned aside from prayer, aware only of the forest round the city.

He was filthy with dust and blood. His palms were sore where he had gripped the iron. He hated iron. He loved the grain of wood, flowing in one direction like barley after a wind. He loved the crackle of vellum in his hands, the muster of black numbers. He loved the shieldlike shapes of light on stone, as in the chapel now, the late afternoon spilling through the high windows.

The candle shadows of the Virgin's gown shifted as the door opened and a cheese-breathed deputy creaked at his side. The man's wait was as insistent as a cat at a door. Geoffrey lifted an eyebrow.

"The king's steward, my lord."

"What!" Geoffrey stood. "Where?"

"He's waiting in the—"

"Here!"

Candlelight on chain mail. A frightened eye. "Waiting in the Meeting Chamber, my lord—"

Why? Geoffrey nearly said aloud, but he strode across the alternating shafts of sunlight and darkness and blinked in the courtyard as he began to run.

A surprise visit. A dove clattered through the air above the dovecot. Eyes acknowledging that yes, the king's man was here, and yes, this was very unusual and something must be wrong. Even the smith's rear end and his grunt as he lifted the hoof of a gelding seemed to indicate that word was everywhere.

"If you hadn't been in such a hurry to—" The deputy who met him could not say "to pray," because it was only proper a victorious hunter should offer thanks. Geoffrey threw a chair out of his way. "Find Hugh," he began, but Hugh was at his side.

Water sang into a bowl. Hugh's white hands released a clasp. The pig stink, a stink like urine, was sharp. He splashed water onto stone. "He's never sent a steward unannounced. Never!"

He stood with dripping hands while Hugh toweled him. "I'll wear my gown with the lilies—no, that would be stupid. Too sumptuous. And he'll be all mud-freckled. Tell me, is he mud-freckled?"

"Somewhat, my lord. Tired, but insisting on seeing you."

"Of course. Has he fed?"

"He wants to see you first."

"Of course," Geoffrey said again, although a new kind of fear made him gaze upwards, into the tapestry of the knights crossing lances, one of them pierced through his eye slits, and slumping forwards, forever leaning, like a man looking for a coin on the ground.

"Perhaps this one, my lord," suggested Hugh, offering the green tunic with the gold trim.

"Yes, and the ornamental spurs. Good. And that sword, with the jet insets. We want to seem comfortable, but manly."

The mirror had a flaw, a rill, like a stone shelf under smoothly flowing water. The fold in the glass bent his reflection, and Geoffrey knew that this was how he must look to the Virgin, who saw him not as he looked but as he was.

The sword swung comfortably at its chain, and Geoffrey withdrew it to test its gleam. "We want to seem capable of war but disdainful of rough play."

Hugh's touch adjusted the cloth round him and tugged a wrinkle out of his stocking. "It's a good thing I was out on a hunt. If I had been here, I would seem a clerk, a do-nothing. To make him wait makes him realize that I am a man going forth into the shire, breathing its air and surveying its cattle." The deep hope that this was, in fact, what he would realize gave Geoffrey sudden confidence.

He struck the hilt of his sword with his palm and glanced in the mirror one last time. He turned smartly. "So."

He hesitated in the corridor, adjusting the sword chain, and was aware of a shadow behind him. He turned, and the shape slipped back behind an arch.

Geoffrey stifled a curse, marched down the corridor to the head of the stairs, and spun.

A figure marched stiffly, threw itself back on its heels, and gawked up the hall just as Geoffrey knew he must be gawking, and Geoffrey drew his sword in fury.

The figure leaped into the air at the hiss of the sword and cowered in a caricature of terror.

Eleanor had insisted. She had said that all the noble families in France had a Fool. She said it would make the castle merrier. For six months the Fool had caricatured Geoffrey, always Geoffrey, no one else. It was apparently his avowed duty to ridicule his employer. Furthermore, he never spoke. Dressed in stockings and a motley tunic, he pranced—never walked—and initiated raucous laughter wherever he went, frowning and thrusting his head forwards.

Geoffrey sheathed his sword. Immediately the Fool was on his feet, at mock attention, eyes screwed shut in an effort of obedience. "You're not funny!" spit Geoffrey.

The Fool nodded in eager agreement.

"You're not good at what you do! You fail to be an effective Fool!"

More eager nods, body quivering with attention.

Growling, Geoffrey turned and suffered the Fool to follow him with God knew what exaggerated gestures and twitches down the spiral stairs.

A jangle of mail and squeak of leather. A youthful messenger began to speak, squeaked, and cleared his throat. "The abbess to see you, my lord."

Geoffrey fumbled his way up a step. "The abbess!" he whispered. Then, sternly: "Explain that I have a meeting, and ask her to wait—" Where? Where could such a woman wait? And more important, where did he want to see her? "Have her wait in the East Tower." There were books there, breviaries foxed with yellow stars, and a Book of Hours, a modest library, but it had a certain dignity. No one would gossip about her meeting him there. An abbess belonged with manuscripts. And the room was private.

She should not have come here. He gazed through the window slit. A hay cart creaked across the stones. The smith's elbow gleamed in shadow, working the bellows. Not here, to this hive.

The chief huntsman gestured before the miller beside the grain kiln. He raised his arms to show the size of the boar's head, or perhaps the size of another boar, or another creature altogether. Doves dodged in and out of the holes in the small tower built for them, the white and pale gray birds looking, at this distance, no more beautiful than lice.

14

4

"A good iron point will take a boar out of his life quick enough," said Ivo.

Hugh was disappointed. He wanted more praise for Geoffrey, his master, the man who was, rightfully, the purpose of Hugh's life. "The lord sheriff never blinked or even twitched, even when the beast blew blood."

"It's best to get them that way—into the heart and lungs, so their blood flows into their wind." Ivo hefted a wooden sword and balanced it in his hand. Then he stabbed with it, into the darkness of his shed. Ivo knew all about swords. He tempered them, repaired them, and knew all that they could do. The old man was strong; his muscles were lively in his forearm as he smiled at the practice sword.

"I've seen my share of blood," said Ivo. "Here's your sword."

Hugh took the blade, a wooden weapon heavy enough to hurt and even kill, but intended to develop the arm and the eye in swordplay. "You could use a sword like this against a boar," said Hugh, cutting the air with a vicious half-circle.

"And get stretched out in a blink. Don't think too highly of a sword, wooden or steel, Hugh. It is a gentleman's weapon, and a pig is no gentleman, now, is he?"

Ivo braced himself on what were plainly strong legs and lifted a battered wooden sword. He made a fierce cry, a cry like a legendary berserker, although the people in the courtyard did not bother to glance in his direction. There was tension in the air—the sheriff was meeting with Baldwin, the king's man.

Ivo's sword fell, and Hugh forced it away. Again, the two-handed blow fell, and Hugh danced to one side, his feet whispering through scattered straw. Ivo did not hesitate. Using all his strength, he tried to pound the weapon from Hugh's hand. The sound of their swords made bright, satisfying cracks.

Hugh began to attack on his own, trying to drive Ivo backwards with great sweeping cuts. Ivo waved Hugh's blade aside each time, sweat beginning to shine on his forehead. The wooden broadswords were heavy enough and, like their steel counterparts, not made for continual work.

Hugh made no progress against Ivo. Hugh's defense was skilled enough, but Ivo was stronger. At last Hugh let his sword arm drop and shook his head. "I need to rest," he said, panting.

Ivo mussed Hugh's hair. "A Mussulman wouldn't let

you rest. He'd cut you into dog snippets, wouldn't he? But you're getting better. Much better. Even an old crust like myself would have a few minutes' trouble with you."

"A few minutes," said Hugh. This was hardly enough. He wanted to be knightly, capable of great deeds.

"Let's go again," said Ivo after a few moments. Again, their wooden blades flashed. Hugh smiled with the effort and with pleasure. He enjoyed this! Anyone would. Rough play, with an old swordsman like Ivo, after a day of such tremendous hunting.

This time Hugh fought better. Ivo smiled his encouragement, backing against the stone wall and flicking aside Hugh's blows, with an occasional lunge of his own.

Hugh's life before coming to the castle had been gray and without laughter. His mother had died at Hugh's birth, and his father, an expert greaver, had worked late every night on leg armor for gentlemen until the dust of metal and the cold nights began to hammer at his lungs. He took to his bed with an icy sweat, and he died blessing his only son.

The priest had squinted at Hugh and taken him into the home for those children who had been provided by God—an all too common burden. There were dozens of orphans, waiting to be apprenticed to dyers or glaziers or to tradesmen who needed another human back to heft sacks of meal. When Hugh showed a steady temperament and a good memory for prayer, the priest's squint became thoughtful, and one day when Hugh was already tall and broad-shouldered, he stood before the lord sheriff, hearing himself praised as unusually quick to learn, "with an uncommon sense of when not to speak, and well versed in his praise of Our Lady."

"The need for copyists here is really not so great," said the sheriff, a man with thoughtful eyes and a short dark beard.

Hugh was weak with disappointment.

"We have quite enough ink-fingered clerks," the sheriff continued, as Hugh felt his last hope wither.

"What I need is a squire," said the sheriff.

It was very unlikely that a lord sheriff would choose the son of a greaver to be a squire. Squires were nearly always the sons of knights, young men with futures who needed training in arms and responsibility.

"What is the lad's name?"

"Hugh," said the priest, in the same way one answers with the age of an already too-leggy lamb.

"Hugh," said the lord sheriff. It was the first time Hugh had heard his name spoken in the castle. It sounded like a strange word, not worthy of the sheriff's tongue. Why, he wondered, could I have not had a more graceful name? Hugh was a quick, plain name. Surely the sound of his name itself was against him.

Now, hacking with wooden swords with Ivo, Hugh felt that he was the luckiest young man in God's world. He could not be happier. This time it was Ivo who laughed, panting, and let his arm fall.

"Enough!" said Ivo.

They sat, wiping their brows with woolen sleeves.

"Remember," said Ivo at last, "the stab is always more effective than the hack. But it's not half the fun, is it?"

That evening Hugh ate his brown bread in the corner of the servants' hall. He was hungry, and the dark beer tasted good. He was so hungry he did not notice the slim figure beside him, and he bumped a slender hand as he reached for the cheese.

"I do hope you are finding quite enough to eat, squire," said the young woman beside him.

He never knew what to say to Bess. She was the personal servant to Lady Eleanor and had an accent very much like a Parisian accent, at least as far as Hugh could guess. He had heard one or two Parisian tradesmen visiting with the sheriff, but their accents sounded, to Hugh's ear, more authentic. He guessed that Bess had been no closer to Paris than he had, but everything else about her was very real. She was dainty, soft-spoken, and cool. And beautiful, in a way that stupefied Hugh.

"Yes, quite enough, and I thank you for your concern," Hugh answered, attempting a dash of court talk.

She did not bother to respond. Men and women of the castle spoke in a stylized way, not at all straightforward like the draymen and foresters of the world beyond. Talk was a game. Hugh was not very good at it.

"You missed a fine day's hunting," said Hugh, hearing his own thorny accent and hating every syllable.

"I did not miss the hunt. My lady and I rode forth on a hunt of our own, as you saw, and we had no interest in that monster carcass, although I am not surprised such rough sport amuses you."

Hugh hid behind his silence. Even imaginary responses sounded inept in his mind. He was happy to leave the hall and happier to leave the cool stone of the castle and slip into the streets of the town.

He would never learn to banter with a young woman like that. And it was banter that won a woman. Talk. Unless you could talk well, you were worthless. Hugh felt thin and futile.

"It's the lord sheriff's squire," said a voice.

The streets were empty and only slightly colored with faint candlelight from the dwellings. In the doorway of The Vixen was a knot of men. Hugh smiled at the faces as he grew close enough to recognize them. But the faces had smiles that were not quite kind.

"The lord sheriff," said the voice, and Hugh recognized Thurstin, the miller's son, a very large yellow-haired young man. Thurstin's father had beaten him when he came home drunk, until lately. Thurstin had reached his full height and strength, and his father had given up. The beatings had done nothing to Thurstin except amuse him and make him impervious to pain of any sort. He had bragged that the horns of a bull would break off before they so much as scratched him.

Since he had begun using the bow and arrow with the belief that he could find service with the king someday, Thurstin did not drink as much. Now he was the only man without a tankard and the only man who spoke to Hugh. "The lord sheriff," he repeated. "Our lord sheriff is the man who spends so much time in the garden. Studying religious matters."

There was laughter. Hugh knew he was being taunted but did not understand, exactly, the nature of the taunts.

He shouldered his way past Thurstin's bulk and regretted being in a room where all faces seemed too amused.

When Hugh had a tankard of ale, he turned and found Thurstin watching him with a mocking grin. "The lord sheriff attends his business, on his knees in the abbey garden, while his squire, son of a bootmaker, holds his horse."

There was more laughter. Hugh was hot. He understood enough: the lord sheriff was being, in some obscure way, insulted, as was Hugh himself. But Thurstin was a great blond bullock—the biggest man in the room.

The ale tasted of sour milk. Sour goat's milk. Hugh shouldered his way, carefully, deliberately, into the street. Hugh knew these men, every one. They were good men, and not cruel. What did they know that Hugh did not?

Thurstin's laugh was loudest as Hugh made his way up the winding street towards the castle gates.

5

The steward to the king ran a broad pink hand through his white hair. "Geoffrey, Geoffrey, I'm afraid. I am truly afraid." Baldwin FitzGilbert stopped, taking pleasure in his silences, as well as in his voice. "I'm afraid I have bad news."

"Please sit down," said Geoffrey, careful to keep his accent clean of any of the northern lichen that had grown on it.

Baldwin lifted a hand and closed his eyes as a way of saying, "Thank you, I am more handsome when I stand." He did place his hands on the back of a chair and moved it slightly, so that it groaned on the stone tiles. This act claimed sovereignty over the objects in the room, and as he acted as agent of the king, it indicated that the king himself had moved the chair, and would move it again, and any other object in the room, as he so desired. Geoffrey had been raised to see what was being displayed at once. The king's will stood upright in the light of late afternoon and leaned against the chair.

"The king," said Baldwin at last, "is displeased."

This was the worst thing that could be said. Geoffrey leaned against the table, when he could move, and studied the fine grain of the oak.

"The king is unhappy with what he learns from this city."

Geoffrey blinked. "I am his eyes here, and his ears." He stopped himself. The king could pluck these eyes, trim these ears, and grow others. Geoffrey took a deep breath.

"He is unhappy with what he learns about his High Way."

The High Way ran south, all the way to London. It belonged to the king as a man's arm belongs to the man. The road was an expression of the king's will, as this man was an expression of his will. The king's agency traveled like a vine over the land and peopled itself in men like Baldwin, as the flesh of Christ multiplied itself in the Blessed Sacrament.

Baldwin waited to see if Geoffrey would display remorse, or incompetence. Geoffrey returned his gaze.

"He is concerned about what he hears about travelers on his road."

Geoffrey groped for a memory.

"About travelers not having free passage along the road."

"Highwaymen," Geoffrey prompted, relieved. "I

knew it!'' This was a mistake. If he had known it, the problem should not have existed, but Geoffrey added quickly, ''I am as concerned as he is.''

''Not highwaymen.'' Baldwin closed his eyes and said as in prayer, ''Geoffrey, not highwaymen in general. But a particular highwayman.''

There were so many, Geoffrey nearly said.

''That particular robber who waylays people. People on the king's business. And demands a toll. As if the road were his!''

Geoffrey shivered.

''Stealing, thereby, not only the tax the king would collect, if he so desired, but the road itself!''

''The king's taxes have been paid on time,'' Geoffrey said, running a fleck of dust off the table with his finger. ''And in full.'' He looked up for confirmation.

''So far. So far, Geoffrey, but while he continues in his faith in your power to collect the money that is his, he worries that you have lost his road.''

Geoffrey bowed his head. The king's men were bits of the king's body. A hazard on the way was like a paralysis, and in this case, it was also an insult, implying that the marriage of king to country was invalid, a thing to be mocked. Mockery was a terrible thing. Geoffrey shook his head in disgust.

Baldwin lifted a hand, as if in benediction. ''Be at ease, Geoffrey. The king stands in faith with you; he trusts you as he trusts his toes to do his bidding.'' Baldwin looked away, no doubt displeased with the image of toes, raising, as it did, the picture of a king wiggling his naked feet. The broad hand fell gently to the back of the chair. "He knows that this problem will be resolved. He knows that you will apprehend the body of this outlaw and deliver justice upon it."

Geoffrey was struck by the well-formed speech of this Londoner, ripe, as it was, with the influence of French and the influence of decades of Latin study, the beautiful pagan masters Geoffrey could read only with difficulty. "Let there be no doubt—" Geoffrey began.

Baldwin waved him silent with an easy gesture. He closed his eyes. "No need. No need." He dropped, as if exhausted, into the chair. "There are many men seeking honor in the south. I speak as a friend now. As a man who knew your father." Baldwin massaged his large, square chin. It was like seeing a priest immediately after mass and finding him weary and human, scratching beneath his cassock. "There are dozens of men who would love to be sheriff of Nottingham."

Geoffrey poured wine from the silver pitcher. The clear green wine was too tart for Baldwin's soft London mouth, and the steward rolled his lips into a knot. Geoffrey lowered his cup, feeling it discourteous to savor such an unworthy wine.

Baldwin drank and touched a cloth to his lips. "I know that you are a gifted administrator." He looked into his empty cup, and Geoffrey filled it at once. "The king appreciates this." The key words were *gifted* and *appreciated*. *Gifted* meant that God had endowed his talent. *Appreciated* meant that the king had appraised Geoffrey as one appraises cloth and knew his value. "But we both know that you are not overfond of wilderness."

Geoffrey drank but did not taste.

"Not that you are cowardly. A crisp, worthy man."
Worthy in the mouth of a man like Baldwin was a deep
compliment. It summarized all that was esteemable
among men. To be worthy was to have weight, as gold
has weight. "But administer the forest as well as you
administer the city."

This combination of praise and criticism made the
criticism all the more scalding. To defend himself would
be craven. Geoffrey stood and stepped to the lintel and
stared briefly at the granite. The quartz flecks glittered
in the late-afternoon sun.

"I will," said Geoffrey at last.

That simple answer made Baldwin clasp his hands
and close his eyes. "I know you will."

This meant that Geoffrey might fail but that Baldwin
was still a friend. "We hunted boar this afternoon," said
Geoffrey lightly. "It threw itself upon my spear and ran
to the cross-shaft just as they are supposed to do."

"They have so much courage that they are stupid."

"I have seen them outsmart the spear," Geoffrey
offered.

"I am like you, Geoffrey. I have little use for blood
gluttony. This age of men loves shouting, and the chase,
and the hacking of flesh."

He refused to acknowledge Geoffrey's feat. Geoffrey
was puzzled. And annoyed. He did not feel much in
common with this soft court steward. "It's important
for the city to see the king's man holding a steady spear."

Baldwin tossed a hand in agreement.

"We interrogate a thief tomorrow."

"Not a highwayman," Baldwin chided, with a smile.

"No," Geoffrey conceded. But he wanted this agent of the king to know that Geoffrey FitzGodse pursued the breakers of the king's law with a hungry sword. "A common street thief. But word is that he has hidden some treasure, no one knows where. We will find it."

"I have seen enough men racked."

"My man has a new method. I'm very curious as to its effectiveness."

Baldwin held forth his cup. "You have my curiosity aroused."

Good, thought Geoffrey. He poured more wine and wrestled the conversation to nostalgia, tales of Geoffrey's father in the old king's court, tales of shattered lances and sweaty horses, the sort of story Geoffrey always pretended to enjoy. The pretense was always successful, and Baldwin drank wine, growing red and deeper-voiced, describing a siege engine, and a boulder shot from a catapult, and a helmet crushed like an egg so the brains ran like yolk.

Baldwin used the London word for egg, *ey*, not the local *eyren*, his speech reminding Geoffrey of all that was soft about London and all that was coarse about this place.

When Baldwin had been escorted, reeling, down the hall, Geoffrey sent for Henry, his chief deputy. Henry huffed into the room and seized the edge of the table to keep from falling. "Is it all right, sire?"

Geoffrey used a gesture Baldwin had just used, a flick of the hand. It was elegant. He did it again.

"God's Lips, sire, why is he here?"

"Don't worry, Henry. You're all flushed."

"I ran up the stairs."

"We needn't panic. The visit was sudden but not unpleasant."

"I'll tell the men to relax. We were so worried—"

Geoffrey was touched at their loyalty, although of course, a new sheriff would need new men. "Henry." The sound of a man's name did have a strange effect on him. It silenced and drew attention like a dirk from its scabbard. "Henry, I need the name of that highwayman."

"Highwayman, sire?"

"That—you know the one. The one that waylays people as a prank. Collects a toll from them. As a joke." Geoffrey hated jokes. Even as a boy he had hated those boys in the back pew who made fart noises as a hefty franklin sat down. Geoffrey's response to a joke was to overlook it. He had overlooked this prankster on the High Way, knowing that he was less a robber than a jester.

"Yes," said Henry, "I've heard of him."

"What do people call him?"

Henry bunched his mouth, searching his memory. "I think they call him Robin."

"Robin."

"I remember: Robin Hood."

"Robin Hood," Geoffrey repeated, with emphasis on the second name.

"Yes, I think so, sire. Do you mean that he is what all of this is about?"

"I know. It's amazing. I've ignored him as an unimportant nuisance. That was a blunder. He is a speck in the eye of the king, and he must be removed."

Henry backed towards the door. "I'll have him in no time at all."

"Him," said Geoffrey, "or his head. Either will do."

6

The abbess looked up from the page in her hands. Geoffrey bowed courteously. "Madame Emily," he said, "how can I possibly be of service?"

"My dear Geoffrey, it's so pleasant to see you. I am afraid my mission is a bit mundane."

"Pray elaborate."

"Pigs."

"Ah."

"An invasion of them, just like last June." She laughed through her nose, like a Frenchwoman. "Certainly you remember that, how they rummaged through the hedge and were so terribly naughty, even when we threw stones."

"I remember," he said softly. He had not seen her since that afternoon, nearly four months ago. Her gray habit was crisp and new, and a band of coral ran round her wrist. Every eleventh bead of her rosary was jade, and a golden brooch hung from the beads, engraved with the letter *A*. Round the peak of the *A* ran a crown, and in fine letters, he knew, having come close to it all those months ago, were the words *Amor Vincit Omnia*.

"A very interesting picture," said Madame Emily.

He stepped to her side and looked at the page she held. He fidgeted at the sight of a nude figure, albeit sexless. A creature was displayed on each part of its body, indicating which astrological sign controlled that part of the anatomy. A sheep foraged among the curly hair of the head; a crab clung to the throat, just beneath a bull that peeked out from behind the neck. With a wince, he noted that the androgynous crotch was bejeweled with a black scorpion. "My father assembled this humble collection," he said.

"There are many beautiful things."

"I'm sure the library at the abbey far surpasses this modest assortment."

"It does, of course, but step over to the light to see this lion. Even in the sunset it is so delightful. You can almost see it twitch its tail."

Near the window meant behind an archway, and he walked her to the wall, although careful not to touch her. "Why have you come here?" he breathed.

"Because I had to see you," she whispered. "Besides, pigs did break into our garden and soiled everything."

With a sick feeling in his stomach, Geoffrey knew that the slaughtered boar had caused its brethren to attack. There were spirits in things, just as the spirit in water struggled to escape when it boiled. Did not our Lord cast the evil demons into a herd of swine?

But the sight of her melted him, as heat renders wax. He opened his hand, and slowly, very slowly, his hand approached her cheek, and he touched her.

"You haven't forgotten?" she breathed.

A memory of great pleasure made him tremble. "How could I?" he whispered into her ear, the crisp edge of her veil at his lips.

She had come, as she had now, to complain of pigs, and she had insisted, daintily but with a touch of impatience, that she see the sheriff himself. He had been ready to ride forth, a gentleman attending a gentlewoman, to the sight of the ravaged hedge.

It was another blot upon his soul. And yet her beauty—not youthful beauty, but something riper— had already dissolved him again, here in the East Tower, cold stone beside them, vellum page rattling to the floor.

He wanted to have her here, now, in the quoin formed by the archway and the wall, but the lion on the chest of the naked figure reminded him where he was and who he was. The black scorpion gleamed on the surface of the parchment.

He hadn't forgotten. He would come to her. Yes, the pigs were shameful creatures. Once again he would inspect the hedge. Love did, it was true, conquer all. He kissed the brooch, the gold warm as flesh at his lips.

GEOFFREY WAS GLAD that Hugh could not overhear his love patter with the abbess. And he was glad, too, that

32

Hugh had no thought of the jealousy he felt now, as his wife turned to meet him. Could such a freely lustful man feel so possessive of his wife? Hugh might be moved to ask, if dismay allowed him to speak at all.

Yes, the sheriff would have to answer. Indeed he could.

His wife's dress flowed to the floor, her sleeves reaching nearly as far. The insides of her sleeves were lined with blue silk, embroidered in gold with the pattern of trefoil leaves. Gold circled her neck, and a drape of coral beads fell from one shoulder to the opposite waist, each bead the size of a knuckle, but perfectly spherical. The beads chuckled as she moved to adjust her hair, speaking to her lady-in-waiting in Parisian, "Oh, look, my husband wears green just as I do, as if it were May."

"If I could speak with you . . ."

His wife tossed a shoulder, and they were alone.

"So—" he began.

She made a pout in the looking glass. "You're angry."

"Why did you go fowling this afternoon?"

"Why not?"

He controlled his voice. "For what purpose?"

"My pleasure." Said softly: *myn pay*.

"I told you I did not want to see you in the company of the falconer."

She turned to glance at him. "He amuses me."

Geoffrey paced the room, head thrust forwards. "The man is a lecher."

She lifted an eyebrow.

"People see you riding off to the woods, and they know!"

She touched her lips as if to keep them in place.

"I don't want to see you with him again."

"I will do as I please."

"I will have him killed."

She made kissing sounds, and a wire-haired dog scrambled from under the bed. She roughed its fur. "You are boring."

"I will have his throat cut," said Geoffrey, voice trembling.

"He is the best falconer for a hundred miles. He has the finest brace of thrice-mewed gerfalcons I have ever seen. I was raised with a bird at my wrist. Everyone knows that. Everyone expects a gentlewoman to be able to withstand the eye of a peasant's son. And they expect me to love that touch of blood. That warmth of the fresh-killed squab. They expect it of me. And I do love it. It makes me feel alive."

She studied his clothes, then turned to the dog and ran her fingers over its ears. "I have to do something to amuse myself, now that we no longer amuse each other. Why are you wearing that silly sword?"

"I thought Baldwin would be impressed by such a fine jet hilt."

"It looks like a toy."

"It has a fine edge."

She put down the mirror at that most subtle of threats and allowed the dog to lave her finger with its tongue. She had been such an excellent choice. Moneyed, intelligent, and pretty after the current fashion, a long, slender neck, like a doe, and a plump belly like a woman always just pregnant. "Don't tell me what to do, Geoffrey."

He closed his hand round the hilt.

"You have your . . . companions." She let her voice curl round the word. "And I have mine."

He had only half guessed. Now he knew. He sat. He knew that a man had no choice in what he did. His father had chosen his wife, and his father had chosen his profession. The type of clothes he wore, the sort of thoughts he had were all prescribed, and happily so. There were no uncertainties. But why, with that little margin of freedom they had, did men and women choose to sin?

He laughed dryly. He was not a brave man, but he wanted to be honest to himself, and he was insightful enough to know that his wife and he were, in a way, well matched. Painfully well. Chess-players who had gone to checkmate many times. They had never loved each other.

She fastened a gold clasp round the dog's neck. It was too bright to be the finest gold, but it claimed the dog as a servant of its mistress. "You are giving me a pain in my head."

"I so often do."

"Please leave."

"All I ask is that you not embarrass me."

She fingered the coral beads, and they clicked like a rosary. She had always valued what were called *perre pres*, jewels of price. They were a way of storing wealth, as ale is a way of storing the sun. "That," she said, "is the only way I can hurt you."

7

Geoffrey regretted telling Hugh that he could have the evening free. He missed the young man's presence.

Geoffrey preferred to wear green when he dined. It was important to pay respect to colors. Blue was the color of Heaven. Green was the color of earth, the color, as his wife had said, of May. No one was ever offended by the color green, and Geoffrey sometimes thought it brought good fortune. He needed good luck this evening, dining on boar garnished with steaming squabs. Geoffrey was the son of a baron, and wealthy enough, but it was a strain to have the servers dressed in their finest livery, one stocking green and one patterned with white leaves, and black sleeves that tapered to the wrist so not to dip into the dishes.

Especially when Baldwin, the king's steward, did not

seem to notice. The two wire-haired dogs pranced on the white lace tablecloth and lapped pudding off a silver plate, and the whippet, a white, graceful figure, caught bits of breast meat tossed through the air, but Baldwin chewed, watching only one thing in the entire room, no matter how Geoffrey tried to distract him.

The Fool juggled red balls and made a penny disappear and appear again, a bright stigmata that opened and vanished, a miracle. He stood on his head, on one arm, and made amazing faces.

And worst of all, the Fool frowned, thrusting forth his head, chewing, so that even the servers colored on their way to the table, and Lady Eleanor laughed behind her napkin. Baldwin stared, fat glistening on his chain, then turned to Geoffrey.

Geoffrey opened a hand to say, "You have a question?"

"He acts like you."

"It would seem so."

"What is the purpose?"

"Humor, sire."

"Humor, humor, humor," said Baldwin, closing his eyes. "To cause laughter."

"Yes."

"I have heard that humor is the fashion in Bologna. But laughter is generally conceded to be a sign of empty-headedness."

"I have always thought so," agreed Geoffrey. "I have always detested open-mouthed laughter. Quiet, personal laughter—"

"Is, of course, proper," said Baldwin. "But this fellow—" Baldwin studied the thighbone of a pigeon.

Geoffrey avoided looking at his wife. "It is fashionable to have a Fool," he said.

"Fashion," said Baldwin slowly, in a tone like regret. "When, forgive me, Lady Eleanor, but when loud laughter becomes the fashion, where will it stop? When I was young, everyone was stern. Dogs were stern. Women would rather eat dung than laugh in the street."

"It's a matter of taste," said Geoffrey, sipping wine. "I, for example, prefer to wear green, which—"

"—some people think is a symbol for lightness in love," said his wife.

"I have never heard that," said Geoffrey.

"Oh, I have, Lady Eleanor. I have. I have heard that degree of faithfulness can be told by the lover's sleeve," said Baldwin. "The heart chooses the color it prefers without thinking and betrays itself."

"This is established truth," said Geoffrey's wife, "widely known."

"I have never heard it." The wine was tasteless, and the boar tough. Geoffrey fed a scrap of flesh to the whippet and said, "Laughter, of course, is now the fashion."

"Oh?" said Baldwin, wiping his chin.

"Although God's earth is replete with examples of His goodness." Wine splashed out of Geoffrey's cup. "To mock any part of it is to blaspheme."

The Fool scowled and squinted, a finger held forth into the candlelight.

"He's acting just like you," said Baldwin.

The Fool's eyes shifted back and forth, bright with suspicion. He withdrew his finger and leaned forwards sullenly. Geoffrey crushed the napkin in his fist. In his chamber mirror, the glass with the single flaw, a wrinkle like the trailing edge of an angel's wing, he was always dignified. A hard-eyed, handsome, bearded man. The Fool bunched a fist, trembling.

Baldwin looked long at the Fool and then leaned back in his chair, studying Geoffrey. Baldwin nodded. "He has amazing talent."

Candlelight gleamed off the saltcellar, an earthenware boat as long as a bread loaf, on which perched a gilded swan. Eleanor had brought this, one of the many valuable objects he had married when he married her. A tapestry behind the Fool showed swans floating on a pool the color of blood. The swans intertwined their necks gracefully, in a manner never quite matched by nature.

After dinner a pikeman stirred the water beneath the drawbridge. Grumpy white shapes shook themselves into the torchlight, smearing the water like mustard. "They are so beautiful," cooed Lady Eleanor. "I think that in the entire world there is no more graceful creature."

"Except, perhaps, one or two of the king's horses," said Baldwin.

"Oh, no," said Eleanor. "Horses are loathsome by comparison."

Baldwin made one of his eloquent gestures. Despite his love for wine, his eyes recorded every detail, so he would be able to answer every question the king might ask.

"But these birds are spotless."

There was nothing so prized as spotlessness, and nothing so undesirable as something spotted. This was why the toad was so abhorred; spots erupted on its surface like bubbles in a cauldron, and spots were not merely superficial blemishes. They betrayed the nature of a thing, testified to a creature's inner baseness.

"Perhaps," said Baldwin, and Geoffrey was struck by the sophisticated tone of the word. "Perhaps," Geoffrey murmured to himself. Not "percase" or "perchance." "Perhaps."

Eleanor broke off a bit of simnel, fine white bread, celebrated for having not a single speck of bran, and tossed it into the water. Ripples flawed the water, and the torchlight shivered. "As you know," said Eleanor in her prettiest voice, "animals exist to teach us moral lessons."

"There is no question," agreed Baldwin.

"The transformation of the silkworm from larva to butterfly teaches us the Resurrection. And the vulture, which breeds without copulation, teaches us of the virgin birth of our Savior." She let a fragment of simnel drift from her fingers.

"And what lesson do we learn from the swan?" Baldwin said with a smile.

"Oh, many many lessons can be learned from the swan," said Eleanor.

Geoffrey plucked simnel from her hands and tossed a chunk of it to the orange-beaked birds. "We learn that what appears beautiful is not always kind."

"What on earth sort of lesson is that?" snapped Eleanor.

"Look at them snuffling and lunging over the bread," said Geoffrey.

"They're hungry," said Eleanor.

"They are greedy," Geoffrey responded. "Since creatures exist only to teach us a moral lesson, we must conclude that the beautiful can be greedy."

"Oh, they most certainly can," droned Baldwin.

"And why are there bees?" Eleanor asked, torchlight gleaming on her teeth.

The lesson of the bee was a commonplace. Bees were obedient to their king, who in turn did not sting them, although he could, if he wanted to. The bee lived in a society of mutual obligation, just as men did. But Geoffrey knew this was not the lesson Eleanor referred to. Since she had not been trained to have original thoughts, he searched his memory for the lessons children were taught when they were learning the natures of the four winds and the shape of the firmament that lay behind the stars. "Why?" he asked.

"To teach us that spite kills, just as the act of stinging kills the bee, dragging out its heart."

"An admirable lesson," said Baldwin.

8

Geoffrey frowned over the paper in his hands. All his servants were entitled to eat in the "house," and the upper servants received candles—not beeswax, but gray tubes that smelled of fat—and candle ends, and wine. They also received a wage. All this in addition to the actual food, and nothing was cheap. The dinner the night before had gone considerably over budget, but times were good, and he could afford it, especially if the result of such hospitality could be the good favor of the king.

Geoffrey felt at home with lists of numbers, with calculations like the ones in his hand, a long line of black numbers reporting from the larder and the buttery. He could imagine the activities of the world round him from lists of figures; just as ice crystallizes round a single pine needle, a vision of the world composed itself round a line of black numbers.

He knew all the taxes owed on every grazing ox, and every sheep, and all the money already collected. He hung at the center of the shire's economy like a benign spider. He knew how many war-horses there were, how many palfreys, and how many carucates of land lay side by side, tawny with barley. He was the king's tax collector, the king's purse strings, and he paid the money he collected into the Royal Treasury, a process that satisfied him just as flattening a slug of white iron must satisfy the blacksmith. He was good at what he did. It was what he had neglected that had risen against him like a viper.

Henry shrugged his shoulders to ease the weight of leather and mail. He breathed the sweet stink of ale and had the cheerful confidence of a man who might well be a drunkard. He swayed slightly as he spoke. Men had ridden forth last night, he was saying. Turned out beds. Demanding the whereabouts of the prankster. No idea yet, but they'd find him. They'd find him if they had to roast a few swineherds over coals.

We should raise the taxes on silk, thought Geoffrey. Too many millers thought themselves worthy of a bolt or two of the elegant stuff, and it gave them an inflated idea of their value to God. Because in a time of prosperity the miller was as crude as ever but had money. He looked up dimly. "What?"

"We'll find him, sire. Rest your mind on that."

Geoffrey fell back in his chair. "You did *what* to peasants?"

Henry straightened his leather armor, which seemed to fight him as he spoke. "We just made an impression, sire."

"I want you to find him, not breed animosity in every hut under the sun."

But Henry was inexperienced at finding outlaws in the forest, Geoffrey knew. Henry swore the miscreant's head would be on a pike within two days, but it was bluster. Geoffrey put his finger to his lips, and Henry fell silent.

"My men are used to city crimes," said Geoffrey. "Their method is to go about pounding doors and racking the truth out of the wretches who won't talk."

"We'll catch him—"

"We need someone who is experienced in the chase. And in the attack. Someone war-hardened."

Henry put his hand to his hilt to demonstrate the way he would slaughter the highwayman.

"Find me Sir Roger," said Geoffrey. "There's a man who fought the Saracen. A man who is notched with battle. He'll have a trick or two for us. Go find him."

Henry hurried away with a jingle of mail.

"That's the way to do it," Geoffrey said to the remainder of his breakfast, bread sopped with white wine. "Use craft, not force."

Hugh offered a dark blue cloak as a way of reminding Geoffrey, but Geoffrey nodded that he did not need to be reminded. For an official duty like this he dressed like a man ready for battle, although lightly armored. A skirt of leather plate hung to his knees, and his sleeves were tight. He worked his fingers into heavy war gloves, although there would be only symbolic battle this morning.

Hugh buckled a sword round him, the weapon of a

nobleman but more than decoration. The jet-handled sword had been keen. This was keen and heavy, so even the flat of it could break a skull. It was tedious that a sheriff had to be dressed like a man ready to kill.

The courtyard was a pattern of sunlight, and men stepped from shadow into light like angels growing from spiritual to concrete beings, arms and legs brilliant, suddenly, mail and armor studs glittering in the sun. A dog yapped. A horse looked out from the stable, sun touching its nostrils. Every peaked roof had a chimney, and a cluster of chimneys, although only the kitchen chimneys exhaled smoke into the blue sky. One dove nudged another out of the dome-shaped openings of the dovecot, and the chapel stood in its own shadow like a building of ice in the puddle of its own making.

Like all the buildings, the prison was built against the wall, its black, rectangular windows looking out over the courtyard like all the buildings, the stones of many different sizes and shapes, and all the various shades of gray, all adding up to hard, strong edges. It could be a dining hall, or a great hall, or a lord's chamber, like the buildings across the courtyard.

Baldwin was dressed like a man ready to ride, a blue tunic, a red riding cape, a cap in his hands. A torch sizzled on the wall, and Baldwin paced to warm himself. "I am indeed curious," he said, his brass spurs tinkling as he paced. "Although I hope the method is a quick one."

"We don't know. It could be quick, or it could be slow," said Geoffrey, looking round for Nottingham, the executioner.

A step whispered in the corridor, and a figure's breath steamed in the torchlight. A soft voice offered courteous greetings, and a lean face came towards them, shadows spreading across it like black fingers. "This should be a very interesting procedure," said Nottingham.

"Quick, I hope," said Baldwin.

"Ah." Regret. Sadness, even. "It may not be so quick."

Baldwin gathered his cape. "Then let's begin."

"The newness of the method is its prime advantage," said Nottingham, his voice so soft it was barely audible. He led the way as they stepped from hissing torchlight to darkness to torchlight, and then their steps echoed down spiral stairs. "The prisoner will not know what to expect."

"That is usually a disadvantage," said Baldwin.

"Anticipation is everything," offered Geoffrey.

"Usually," said Nottingham. "But this prisoner is very stubborn."

He used the word *thro* for "stubborn," a word that Baldwin might not understand, so Geoffrey said, "Stiborn," a word so often applied to farm animals. "Like a beast, and as stupid."

"Yes," said Nottingham. "If he anticipates the agony, he will harden himself against it. Of course, hardening against agony is a waste of time. We know that. They don't."

An executioner was always named after the city in which he worked. Nottingham had another name, given to him by his father, but because he inherited the position from his father, no one ever called him anything else. He did the city's bidding, he acted on its behalf, and whenever he lifted an axe or built a gallows, he acted as the city, a man who gave the city arms, legs, and a rope.

A dark cloak whispered, the color of water under a drawbridge, black tinged with green. Manacles rattled. A slack face, with dark eyes, like the eyes of a mouse. The dark cloak the prisoner wore made him blend with the darkness. His face and hands floated like bread on water.

A hiss of cloth, and the cloak pooled on the floor. The naked prisoner was pale as tallow, his pubic hair black, a pinch of night. He did not struggle against the black leather gloves of the guards, but his eyes searched the floor. He was trying to find the place in himself that would feel no pain, like a man searching for a forgotten word.

Nottingham tested the straps, then knelt beside the prisoner. He whispered into his ear the words that implored him to divulge his secrets to the mercy of the king.

"There is no treasure," said the prisoner.

Nottingham rose slowly. A torch behind them made a long, slow sigh, like a sleeping dog. Nottingham ran a forefinger along the white flesh of the prisoner's thigh.

Geoffrey nodded his permission to proceed. Any treasure found buried would be returned to its rightful owner, if such an owner could be found. But most of it would slip into the king's purse. Geoffrey wanted the entry in his books: "tresoure founden."

A gate clanked, and a rope snaked into the light,

followed by two horns. The rope slumped to the floor for a moment as four legs struggled to stand on the cold stone. The prisoner closed his eyes as a knife no longer than a finger, and graceful, like a feather, made a slice in the sole of his foot.

The rope was wrestled into a hard knot, and the goat's snout pressed against the blood. The goat shivered with the effort of pulling away and failing. Then a sound like a dog lapping milk.

The goat lapped the cut on the prisoner's foot.

"The king holds forth his hand to you, his beloved son," whispered Nottingham.

The prisoner grimaced.

"He begs you to tell what you have hidden from his sight, so that you may obtain mercy."

The prisoner whipped his head back and forth, with a flash of teeth.

"He waits in sorrow for the words of one of his children."

Baldwin ran his fingers through his hair and crossed his arms. The steady lapping of the goat was like dripping water, ceaseless and strangely comforting, like rain.

A cry. Scalding. Geoffrey stepped back and covered his ears. Such noises could damage the ears, he believed. It was best to preserve the senses. Deafness was a blight.

Baldwin said something, and Geoffrey uncovered his ears. Baldwin spoke again, but still Geoffrey could not hear. "Very impressive!" shouted Baldwin.

As always, weeping. Howls. Words that made no sense. The lapping of the goat inaudible now, the gray tongue working deep into the sole.

Baldwin nodded. Geoffrey knew that the king would hear good reports from this city and was thankful. Mary had been merciful, and he had been spared total humiliation.

The straps squeaked at the prisoner's wrists. Nottingham knelt beside him, whispering. Then screams again, enough to make Geoffrey blink and gesture the suggestion that they go upstairs. Baldwin shrugged and followed Geoffrey, looking back again at the white body, which glistened now with sweat.

The mind was nothing. Thoughts were illusions, knowledge so much smoke over a courtyard. The body was all that mattered. The court of the Kingdom of God was a part of Christ's body, the head, the arms, and legs, and nails, joined to Him. And so a man's soul was joined to his body, and to reach the soul, the body had to be shoveled aside, like so much earth, by fasting, by self-imposed discomfort, or, in this case, by the lawful ministrations of the king's servants.

A smile, a courteous expression of thanks, and Baldwin and his red-caped retinue clip-clopped across the drawbridge. Geoffrey stood, hand on hilt, as if his hand had found comfort in the knowledge that he could butcher a man on the spot, and then, as soon as Baldwin was out of sight, Geoffrey hurried to the prison.

"Stop it!" shouted Geoffrey.

Nottingham's lean face gaped upwards.

"That's enough!"

The goat's tongue lapped air, and then the beast was dragged kicking into the darkness.

"There is no treasure," said Geoffrey.

"Can we be sure?" whispered Nottingham.

Executioners enjoyed a special status. They were shunned, ignored, loathed even, and yet they, too, were agents of the king. They could even question the sheriff, and the sheriff had to suffer their impertinence. There was treasure somewhere. Geoffrey was certain of it.

"Yes. We can be certain that there is no treasure. This wretch would have told us by now."

Nottingham's face turned into the torchlight, stiff with an expression so much like contempt that Geoffrey looked away. "I'll have this man returned to his cell," said Nottingham.

"Do so."

"I will interrupt the interrogation and have him taken to his cell."

"Yes."

"He will be hanged tomorrow, and we will never know where the treasure is."

"That is correct," said Geoffrey.

"Very well, sire," whispered Nottingham, as he stepped into the darkness like a figure dissolving.

9

"S ir Roger is here," said Hugh.

"Good. Ask him in."

"He did not want to come," said Hugh, bringing a second chair to the meeting table.

Geoffrey did not want to see him, either. The lean face of Nottingham and the white nakedness of the prisoner had made him feel something he had not felt before, and he wanted to sit on the sill of the window and watch men come and go.

The thoughtful stride of the doctor across the courtyard told him that Lady Eleanor had yet another headache or perhaps one of those strange weaknesses in her legs. The doctor wore blood-red, slashed with blue, and the lining was shiny taffeta. His boy accompanied him, carrying a large black basket, drugs, roots, powders, and leeches, as Geoffrey knew from his own brushes with illness.

"He was so busy with his studies that he said he had no time for any business but God's."

"Sir Roger said that?"

"According to Henry."

"That doesn't sound at all like Sir Roger. He's been keeping to himself lately, but he's always been a good man at meat and drink. Filled with stories from the East."

A kitchen wench leaned a huge black tub against a wall, went back inside, and came out with a large brush.

Sir Roger found his way to the chair but remained standing.

"I hate to trouble you in your studies, Sir Roger, but I need a man with experience in handling the attack."

Sir Roger did not speak for a long time. The air was touched, for a moment, with the spice of horse manure. "The attack on what?"

"Miscreants."

Sir Roger turned away, shaking his head. He folded his age-knobby hands and said, "I'll do no more damage to my immortal soul than I have done."

Geoffrey waited for more, but when he heard only the chime of the smith's hammer across the courtyard, he said, "Your soul must be the most precious gem in the kingdom."

"Black as tar. I have been studying."

Studying was a well-known form of mortification, like fasting, but more difficult.

"When angels appear to mortal men, it is in the guise

of youthful eunuchs," Sir Roger continued. "Beautiful youths, brighter than the sun."

Geoffrey covered his eyes with his hands.

"They are clad in divine garments. Gold and white silk, and their hips and knees shine like green grass and citron." The old knight groaned as he sat. "I have a Saracen arrowpoint in my thighbone. A black tooth in my timber."

Geoffrey turned to the window. A cartload of wood creaked across the stones below, pulled by two oxen that looked out upon the bustle of the castle with eyes that understood and forgave.

"Exactly so do the sins of my youth anchor themselves, black and rusting, in my soul. When we die, we pass twenty-one tollhouses, each manned with a demon smeared with feces and speaking fire. Each represents a sin: slander, envy, falsehood, wrath, pride, inane speech, usury and deceit, despondency coupled with vanity, avarice—"

"This is grievous . . ." Geoffrey began.

"—drunkenness, evil memories, sorcery, gluttony, homosexuality, adultery, murder, theft, fornication, and hardness of heart. I have left some out. Slander, envy, falsehood, wrath—"

"Please stay seated, Sir Roger. A terrible list. But, and I am an ignorant man, it seems that a further sin is to think too much on sin."

"Yes, that, too!" howled Sir Roger.

"I depend on you for good advice, Roger."

"Then I will tell you of the Seven Deadliest."

Geoffrey put his hand on Sir Roger's shoulder. He

released him at once, appalled. The man had wasted. The burly Sir Roger, who had sworn that when knife was in meat and drink in horn he was the best man under the sky, was gone. This skeleton remained.

"Pride," said Sir Roger. "Lechery." Was there a special emphasis in his voice? "Envy. Anger. Avarice. Gluttony. Ah, gluttony." Regret, or nostalgia? "Sloth."

"A terrible list," said Geoffrey.

"A terrible list." Agreement so vehement it was like sarcasm. "How will any of us reach Heaven?"

"Heaven!" said Geoffrey, exasperated.

"God's retinue . . ." began Sir Roger.

"Sir Roger," said Geoffrey, speaking fast, before the old man's mind clouded further, "I need to catch a highwayman who hides in the forest. My men are inexperienced, and I can't race them like a brace of hounds through the woods. Even if I did, they'd fail."

"You think me mad, like that woman by the churchyard."

Geoffrey pulled his sword belt back into place. "May I speak bluntly?"

"You think I should be sealed into a stone tower just like that madwoman, that shrieking hag."

"Some people think her half a saint."

"You think I am like her. I can't sleep. I wake and think: I have wasted my life."

The very phrase appalled Geoffrey. He had never imagined such a thought. How could a life be wasted? He did not want to listen to Sir Roger suddenly and found himself listening to the distant clatter of the smith's hammer, thankful for such a common, simple noise.

"We catch what we want by letting it come to us," said Sir Roger.

The memory of the boar spear made Geoffrey frown and rub his hands together. "How am I supposed to lure this man here?"

"What does he like?"

"I don't know anything about him."

"If he wanted to lure you, what would he use?"

If a man wanted to lure Geoffrey into the forest, he would use women.

"Whatever you do," said Sir Roger, "do not play his game. Play your own."

The concept of the game was very important. Every courtly man understood the importance of the contest as a test of wits and courage and as proof that life itself was a serious game, human souls to the winner.

Sir Roger had been stout. He had killed dozens. He had been to Jerusalem and had despised weakness wherever he discovered it. Even now he seemed strong, but it was a much different strength. Again, Geoffrey laid a hand on Sir Roger's shoulder. "You shouldn't keep to yourself. You should grace these halls with your presence."

"What is that strange man who says nothing?"

"Ah," said Geoffrey.

"I thought, at first, that he was a relative, a brother of your wife's, who has become weak-headed and whom you have taken in."

"No, he is a Fool."

The old man formed the word *Fool* with his lips.

"It is a fashion in Paris. And—and other places. He amuses people."

"He pretends to be separate from human relations, like a ghost."

"Apparently," said Geoffrey.

"Why does he do this?"

"It's his duty."

"But why did he discover *that* duty, of all others? Was his father a Fool? Did a nobleman discover him and teach him to be a Fool?"

"I don't know. I've never asked him."

"Do so. I want to know."

"He never talks."

For the first time Sir Roger offered something like his old smile. "Make him talk."

Long after Sir Roger had gone, Geoffrey watched the kitchen wench bent over her pot. Her arms were bare, and her gray dress flattered the curves of her body as she worked.

He sent for Henry, and when Henry puffed into the room smelling of sweat and wine, Geoffrey spoke without taking his eyes off the girl's white arms. "What does this prankster like most, this Robin Hood?"

"The forest, I suppose, sire."

"I mean, what sport? Feasting? Drinking? Swordplay?"

"I have heard that he draws a good bow."

Geoffrey turned to embrace the robust deputy. "My good Henry! Most prized Henry! You are a gift from God!"

Henry stammered his thanks.

"We will organize an archery contest. With a gold mark for the winner."

This was well within Henry's talents. He hurried off, breathless with enthusiasm for publicizing the contest into the farthest reaches of the shire, into the forest even, to draw those yeomen rarely seen in the city. Archery contests were not uncommon; Geoffrey asked Henry to hold one from time to time to keep the men in condition and to amuse them, although Geoffrey was always slightly bored with such events.

Geoffrey stepped through the water that had flowed from the wash-pot. "My dear," he said softly.

"Oh!" gasped the girl. "You frightened me, my lord!"

Geoffrey gave her his best smile, the smile that was his greatest gift. "You have a beautiful voice," he said.

Blushes. Downcast eyes. Her knuckles were harsh red from her work, and her forearms were beefy. Her eyes, however, were dark, and her lips were red. "We can always use a beautiful voice about the hall. Meet me in the East Tower tonight, after the first watch. I'd like to talk with you further."

The brush was as black as the iron it scrubbed, with thick, sharp bristles. Geoffrey touched the brush, as if to say, "You do not deserve such crude labor; you deserve a place of special honor."

She would be there, she said, her eyes downcast.

"Don't be afraid if it is dark," he said. "I will be there, waiting for you."

10

Hugh tried to read the sheriff's mood, but as so often, Geoffrey's expression told nothing. Hugh ached to learn more about the meeting with the king's steward, but he could not bring himself to ask.

Boys chased hoops, driving them ahead with sticks, and another strode ahead on a pair of stilts. Geoffrey's horse tossed its mane at the sight of the children, and Geoffrey looked back to say to Hugh, "Ivo tells me your swordplay is improving."

The young man colored. "Ivo is a good teacher."

Geoffrey nearly said, You make me proud. But some inner reserve held him back. His own father had been a stern man who had once made a pilgrimage to Rome and felt that praise fed a young man's pride. If I had a son, Geoffrey found himself musing, I would want him to be like Hugh. It was the serious look in his eye that had captured the sheriff from the first. Geoffrey had never regretted taking on a greaver's son, an orphan, as a squire. But to care for someone left one open to possible pain. What if something should happen to Hugh? Geoffrey didn't think he could bear it.

Two rough timbers, three times a man's height, were topped with a cross-beam. Four studs supported the angles: two at the top, two at the bottom. The gibbet stood on a knoll, an announcement of the law's power. In the distance a stream turned a mill wheel as a small white figure stood in a doorway. A magpie, black and white, perched on the cross-beam, looking towards the city, peaked buildings and a spire of chimney smoke that rose into the smoke-colored sky.

The thief would hang here tomorrow, until he rotted. The magpie would be replaced by a flock of carrion crows, black as numbers on a page. They would circle as the body was cut down and gradually turn to other duties.

"Birds teach us what lesson, Hugh?"

"Cheerfulness, sire, and acceptance of our duties."

"Good." And yet there were often shadow lessons, lessons you were never taught but guessed at yourself. A blackbird consuming a man called happily as it worked. "It's important to be cheerful as much as possible. Not too cheerful. Only as cheerful as is proper."

A peasant in a black cap the shape of his skull struck a tree with a stick, and acorns fell to the ground. Pigs ate them, and a dog watched the pigs, sitting alertly as the man worked. The dog was well fed, although a fly tasted a sore on its backbone. Pigs wandered, snouts to the ground, into the trees, where other peasants rested, leaning on their sticks. Branches littered the ground, and the trees were naked stalks until, over a man's height, foliage began. Acorns sprinkled the dirt, each brown tooth capped with the helmet that had held it to the tree.

Geoffrey's horse tossed its mane, but Geoffrey held the horse in, enduring the pig stink and the sight of the expressionless faces of the peasants. How disgusting pigs were.

His horse twitched a fly. The insects craved the presence of pigs, having sprung, by the effect of sun, from pig feces. "I have a special assignment for you, Hugh."

The young man looked grave.

"I want you to stand guard here, watching these pigs."

The walls were the color of parchment, and a crack here and there made them look temporary. The trees near the wall had been trimmed after the current fashion, as if the trunk were a tree's best feature. The golden-leafed branches of fruit trees tangled into the air just over the walls, and in some places red-leafed ivy covered the walls, although the ivy had been pulled away in places, leaving scars like the marks of stitching.

The hedge had indeed been trampled. A fly preened on a day-old pig dropping. Wild roses were squashed, and a privet bush had been destroyed. Geoffrey had little patience with gardens and preferred an embroidered lily to a real one. Still, he could tell destruction when he saw it.

11

He slipped through the trees, leaving Hugh behind. The clearing was littered with leaves as broad as hands. He deliberately pressed one with his foot, and it crackled. He knelt and gathered his brown riding cape round himself. The pupa of a moth clung to a twig beside him, a horned sarcophagus primed for resurrection in the spring.

A woodpecker drilled a tree high above him. Its yellow head was a glint through the branches. The forest was restless with itchy noises. Another leaf paused like a glove on a lower branch, then slipped, palm up, to his knee. She let him wait.

A red slipper kissed the green grass, and Geoffrey stood. "You're late!" he whispered, meaning passion more than impatience, but he meant also that he was thankful that she had come at all.

"I have duties," she said, releasing the clasp beneath her chin. Her wimple hung loose, and she lifted it, disclosing auburn hair that caught the light and kept it, as if itself a source of illumination. "Besides, haste is such an ugly habit."

"I have always despised it," he breathed.

"Everything in its time," she murmured, smoothing back her sleeves to display her white wrists, which Geoffrey kissed slowly, anything but hastily. "The world was made quickly so that we could pleasure in it at our leisure," she said, her voice growing throaty and close to his ear.

The abbess wore a different brooch this time, a small golden sun that was already warm, before he touched it, from touching the cloth over her breast. He kissed it, a surrogate mouth, a kiss that made her shudder.

"You saw what the creatures did?" she said, her throat vibrating at his lips.

A dog snuffled. Leaves crackled. The abbess was wide-eyed. She melted into the shadows. So quickly—she was gone.

At first Geoffrey thought the peasant had a pig by the leash, but the animal wrinkled its snout and showed yellow teeth.

The man pulled the shapeless wool-brown cap from his head. "What are you doing?" Geoffrey spit.

The man uttered a lump of sounds.

"What?"

"Lad sent me along."

Geoffrey curled his lip.

"Said you looked for me, my lord," the man continued, with all the grace of a man letting half-chewed food fall out of his mouth.

"Your pigs," said Geoffrey carefully, "have upset the abbess terribly."

The peasant wiped his mouth with the back of his hand and studied the ground.

"She is nearly mad with horror at what they have done to her garden."

The peasant's chin reached his chest.

"Sick with horror. Unable to carry out her duties, driven by a profound loathing for what"—the pig dog showed its teeth again—"your pigs did to flowers that are intended to give thoughts of Heaven and which that herd trampled into the dirt like so much filth." The dog growled, and Geoffrey drew his sword. The dog lunged.

"Release your dog," said Geoffrey calmly.

"No, no, my lord," cried the peasant. "He's a servant, my lord."

"Let him go!"

"No, my lord," said the peasant, falling to his knees. "He's all I have," or words to that effect, misshapen sounds a turnip might utter if it were given voice.

The sword hissed through the air and lopped a branch off a holly bush. Geoffrey showed teeth. Thus with your dog, he gestured, and thrashed the holly bush to pieces, leaves and twigs raining down upon him as he stood panting.

The peasant knelt, with closed eyes, supplication filling his body and making the smell of him reach Geoffrey, and the smack of peasant after the scent of that gentlewoman was sickening.

"Go," said Geoffrey, and the peasant dragged his dog through the trees. The sheriff heard the crackle of a step.

The sword did not slide smoothly into the scabbard. Geoffrey forced it in and kicked a tangle of holly out of his way.

"Did he find you?" asked Hugh.

"I gave him a stern scolding," said Geoffrey. "I don't know if he understood much. It's hard to know what goes on in the mind of someone like that."

THE GIBBET cast a messy, indistinct shadow, and the birds that perched on the cross-beam became indistinct, too, as they released their hold on it and soared into the air.

12

It was hot in The Vixen. A great stub of wood sputtered flame in the fireplace. The room smelled of beer, and sweat, and smoke, and the ale tasted good, better than the kitchen beer of the castle.

Hugh enjoyed the company of Sam, the innkeeper, a red-faced man who drank his share of his own ale, until a voice broke over Hugh like a staff. "The bootmaker's son, back from his prayers at the abbey."

Thurstin stood in the middle of the room, ruddy with firelight, his hands on his hips. "Back from his lord's pleasure in the abbey garden."

Hugh turned back to his ale.

"Too highborn to share a story or two with a miller's son. A fine squire. Shadow to such a worthy sheriff. Dusting off the sheriff's knees when he's done servicing our local brides of Christ."

Hugh and Geoffrey had ridden back into the castle in silence. Hugh knew what was happening. He had seen nothing, and yet it was clear. The sheriff must think me a boy, Hugh said to himself. He must think me blind. Everyone knows that he and the abbess are—

The thought that the sheriff and Lady Eleanor might not have the happiest of marriages had occurred to Hugh. But now a heavy mixture of embarrassment and pain made Hugh wish he could shrink to a pinprick.

There was laughter. Hugh closed his eyes. May the earth itself open and swallow and chew one miller's son.

"Such a noble squire, right hand to such an honest sheriff he doesn't dare spend a word on us. His words are golden now, aren't they, this fine squireling?"

"Be quiet."

Someone said that. Who? Hugh was aghast to realize that his very own voice had uttered the two words.

The Vixen was silent, except for the spitting of the fire.

"The sheriff's squire has a voice! But I couldn't quite make out what his wee voice had to say, could I? Could it be that our boy is tired from a day's work and can hardly speak like a man? Can it be he's had a taste of the abbess himself? No doubt, it's true with such a worthy master as the lord—"

Hugh's head buried itself in Thurstin's belly. At least it was intended to be buried in Thurstin's belly. The bulk of the blond ox was too great, and Hugh felt himself being picked up and carried like a load of kindling into the cold dark of the street.

Hugh was lifted high into the darkness and thrown into the patch of light cast by the doorway. Thurstin was laughing, an ugly sound from high above.

Hugh knew that he was hurt, and maybe hurt badly, but that pain had not yet begun. He lifted himself on one arm and bit Thurstin hard above the knee.

His teeth sank deep, through hairy wool, into meat, and the wool grew sodden as Thurstin howled, and then Thurstin began to hurt Hugh in a way mere cobbles could not. His great hands picked Hugh up, threw him down, and picked him up again.

Thurstin worked quietly, and when Hugh struck back, his fist bouncing off Thurstin's chest, belly, shoulder, Thurstin grinned.

"He's a worthy man," Hugh gasped. "And you are an ox!" As Hugh fought, he fought for the sheriff and for himself, the sheriff's extra pair of hands. And he also fought for the things he had believed in before this day. He knew the sheriff should not be spit upon by coarse men. He knew for all the sheriff's sins, he deserved the respect of the men of the city, who would not know worthy from unworthy. Everything was false to men like these.

Thurstin laughed and punched all other words out of Hugh until the innkeeper dragged Thurstin away. "That's enough sport for one night," said Sam, and Hugh stood and fell.

"He's a worthy man!" shouted Hugh, but the innkeeper dragged Hugh up the street, into the dark barely tinged with candlelight.

"Best run home before you lose each and every tooth in your head, Hugh."

Hugh swayed, breathing hard.

A GUTTER RAN DOWN the middle of the street, and Hugh followed it. He did not follow it long, until he began to weep. When he was done weeping, he found his way back to the castle gates.

"What misfortune is this, Hugh?" asked the guard.

"I stumbled," said Hugh.

"A bad fall," said the guard, not unkindly. The news would be everywhere by morning, and Hugh felt shrunken as well as filthy.

"It was a fight," said Hugh.

"No doubt the other man looks the same."

"It was Thurstin."

"And you can still walk! Come along, Hugh. That's quite enough adventure for one night."

Hugh tried to sneak through the servants' dining hall, but Bess sat gossiping with the cook. "Look who fell into the privy," she said.

Hugh washed himself in cold water in his bedchamber, a small room next to the sheriff's. When he was clean, there was no sign of a fight, except for the bruises that had already blossomed on his ribs and a gouge inside his lower lip. He looked, in his speckled hand mirror, thin and shaken, with the eyes of a stranger.

He felt empty. Bitterness and anger had both left him. He was exhausted, but he found himself staring at his own bunched fist.

13

ottingham smiled. "You may, of course, talk to the thief, sire, but whatever can such people say? They are little more than animals, as you know."

"Very little more," agreed Geoffrey.

"You have some act of persuasion in mind perhaps?"

"Yes, I do."

"I knew you would change your mind."

It was always night within these walls. A taper illuminated an oak table and the lean face of the executioner as he smiled, looking into Geoffrey's eyes as into the eyes of a man he knew very well and liked. Geoffrey smiled back in return, sharing a chuckle. Yes, he had changed his mind. He wanted the treasure.

"I will show you the way myself."

"Don't trouble yourself. One of your men can lead the way."

"I insist. I have a special interest in this prisoner."

They cast misshapen shadows in the torchlight of the corridors. Iron bars threw thick, trembling shadows into a chamber filled with gray straw. There was a smell of urine and sweat.

"I want to talk with him alone," said Geoffrey.

"Stir yourself," said Nottingham. A hand crept into the torchlight. An eye gleamed. "I can make him talk," said Nottingham. "I can make him do anything, but you must give me time. You can't interrupt a procedure and expect—"

Geoffrey gripped his arm. "Leave us."

"I fear you will simply waste your precious time, my lord."

"Please."

Nottingham bowed. "As you wish." He stared through the bars. "I skinned a man like him once. The thin ones are better than the fat. The fat ones ooze. We don't flay often anymore, do we?"

"No need to."

"I'm glad. Such a messy procedure. But effective. A man will say anything when he has no skin."

Nottingham's steps whispered down the corridor, and Geoffrey knelt, his face against a cold iron bar. "I passed a gibbet today," he said. "It is on a mound of earth, and the view from the top of it must be impressive. It is the very gibbet we will use tomorrow."

Straw rustled. A figure crept into the torchlight but did not meet the sheriff's eye. "Why do you tell me this?" Hoarse and weary. "How can I look forward to my death with anything but hope?"

70

A pretty speech from a thief. "I have an offer for you."

The prisoner did not speak.

"An offer of mercy."

"Why should you show mercy to me?"

"Here is my offer. If you disclose the location of the treasure, I will set aside the sentence of death and order that your hand be cut off instead. In that way you can keep your life, and I can have the money."

"I would rather die."

"You value your fingers so much?"

"I don't trust you."

Bold talk. Geoffrey stood. "You have as much as admitted now that you have a treasure, hidden somewhere. This interests me. I care nothing for you. Nothing at all. You are like a dog on a leash to me, even less."

The man shrank into a heap of dark cloth and said nothing. The pain in his feet was so great he could think only of relief, and hanging meant he would have no more pain. Geoffrey understood this and also understood that the loss of a hand was even more agony. You could not negotiate with someone who wanted to die.

"Ours is an unpleasant job, sire," said Nottingham, as if he had heard every word. "So much depends on us."

Geoffrey did not like agreeing with this soft-voiced man, but it was true. "Proceed with the hanging. There is no choice."

"It is best to show no mercy."

"I have always thought so."

And yet, he thought, crossing the courtyard, stepping

round a spill of fresh manure, he had not always thought so. He had commanded that men be tortured; he had even seen a traitorous tax collector, a man who had conspired to embezzle, lose his eyes, a proceeding that made Geoffrey thankful that such traitors were so rare. He had never questioned the justice of such punishments. But something about them made him feel frail and less sure of himself. No doubt this was yet another secret weakness, another flaw he had to hide.

Someone turned to avoid his eyes and ducked behind the chapel. The falconer. Proof again that the falconer and Eleanor were lovers. As soon as he began to feel the ache less, something refreshed the pain. A goose was driven, honking and peering one way and then another, towards the kitchen. The whippet ran to his hand and tasted his fingers. The Fool balanced a kitchen knife, point down, on his nose, to the evident pleasure of the cooks.

Sir Roger had said, Make him talk.

He would make the Fool talk. He would make him explain everything. But this afternoon he wanted to sit with pages of vellum, and check sums, and perhaps hear a report on sheep or the disease that made the barley grow in patches like mange.

Hugh unbuckled Geoffrey's sword belt. All of this experience, this closeness to a man like Geoffrey, was a priceless education. Hugh knew it and no doubt believed that God had picked him out for this special honor. Geoffrey hated to chide Hugh, but it was his responsibility. ''Sometimes, Hugh, you let an expression of pride show on your face." Hugh's face was swollen, his eyes downcast.

What showed in Hugh's manner today was not pride, after all. I am a mortal man, Hugh, Geoffrey nearly said aloud. A mortal, sinful man.

Why, Geoffrey demanded of himself, did I take Hugh with me yesterday? Why did I allow the young man to guess at my own wayward nature? Don't think ill of me, Hugh, Geoffrey wanted to say. "Are you feeling well, Hugh?"

"Quite well, my lord."

"You're sure?"

If there was going to be a period of shame between them, of averted gazes, it would announce itself now. Hugh met his eyes and said, "Just a little weary this morning, my lord." Geoffrey considered this: Hugh was showing a grown man's care with words.

Geoffrey consoled himself with work.

This was his place. Sitting in a corner of the great hall, wedge of cheese in his hand, listening to a report on the pavage for the city streets, a tax collected to allow the public way to be cobbled. The clerk spoke in numbers, numbers that described the income of the city and its power. Geoffrey listened, feeling that even as they spoke, cobblestones in distant riverbeds began to glow, began to work fitfully to one side or another. Just as the hairs on the head are numbered.

14

It was raining out. The dim pricks of light from three windows glistened on the black paving stones. Everywhere else was black, inside-of-skull black, the black of the deepest point of a scabbard.

His wife crooked a finger, and he entered her bedchamber. She wore a sleeping cap of light gray, a sash across her forehead and a flower at the side, a bright pink too unsubtle to be one of nature's. She ruffled the fur of a dog.

"I've been waiting for you to say something," she said.

"About what?"

"No doubt they will discuss me with the king. Oh, Geoffrey is doing well, Your Highness, but his wife is a tiresome hag who burdens him with a tedious Fool only she thinks is funny, and he can't stand to sit at the table with her."

"Nobody else thinks he's funny?"

"The problem, my dear Geoffrey, is you. You think your own thoughts, have your own opinions, your own worries, and you don't care whether someone right beside you is flayed alive with shame."

Geoffrey began to compose a speech. An apology, blended with a warning that he had many responsibilities.

"You may go," she said.

What could he say? He left her and wandered the corridor aimlessly. He could strangle the dog. He could strangle her. Both pointless activities, which would probably give him very little pleasure.

A familiar figure stood, one arm against a wall, staring down into the black courtyard. Perhaps to be a Fool was to be cursed. Perhaps it was to accept a form of self-denial—to parody the essentially matter-of-fact, to mimic the tedious. But if he destroyed the Fool, he would hurt his wife in a way she would never expect.

The Fool wore a peasant cap, pulled over his head, so that his head resembled a gourd. His tunic was pied, red and black, and his stockings were black and white, a motley that was almost elegant. He had dark eyebrows and bright eyes and seemed to have applied some art to his lips. They were as red as slapped flesh.

"My father loved to laugh," Geoffrey was surprised to hear himself say. "It's strange. In every way I have surpassed my father's accomplishments, and yet he surpasses me in the pleasure he drew from life." The Fool's eyes looked into his own, dark and gleaming, like stones of great price. Geoffrey did not even know if the Fool spoke English or if the Fool was utterly deaf. "You see a lot, but I wonder how much you understand."

The Fool collapsed to the floor, and his feet projected into the air where his head had been, the stout shoes of a huntsman, until Geoffrey examined them closely, which he took the leisure to do, since he had paid for them. Not quite as stout as a huntsman's shoe, thinner-soled, more built for leaping. Green leather, forest green, but unstained. The Fool rarely went beyond the courtyard.

"The world is so much surface. So much exterior," said Geoffrey to the Fool's shoes. "We can never be completely certain what is going on in someone else's mind." For some reason the Fool made him feel like talking, but this was understandable. Some men could open their hearts to a dog.

"I have been encouraged to make you talk. But I detest the idea." Nothing demoralizes like a promise of mercy.

Geoffrey waited the amount of time he would have spent listening to the Fool if the Fool were talking. And in an odd way he *was* talking. By standing on his head in a very relaxed way, the Fool intended to communicate something. Geoffrey tried to guess what. A kind of cheerful insult, of course, but perhaps something else.

"Because we are flesh, cruelty can force us to do anything," said Geoffrey. "When the king wants me to apprehend someone, he simply orders me to bring his body into the keep. His body. Alive, almost always, because justice cannot be visited upon a corpse. What it can be visited upon is the man's soul, but to catch that, you must bring its cage. The body is everything.''

The Fool sprang to his feet in a graceful bound that made Geoffrey step back, startled. The Fool seemed to say that yes, the body was everything and that this was a good thing. See, the body is beautiful. The Fool tumbled across the floor and sprang from hands to feet to hands on down the corridor, a way, Geoffrey supposed, of bidding good evening.

When the tumbling figure had vanished down the corridor, Geoffrey continued to stare after it. The Fool was a mystery, like the mummified serpent with two heads Geoffrey had seen as a boy and actually touched. Tough as spliced cable, with four withered eyeholes and twin rows of fine teeth, barely teeth at all, armor in the mouth. A creature God had thrown down to the earth like Aaron's staff, to say: see, I am God. Heaven and earth pass before me, and I can make anything I desire beneath the firmament.

God, however, had not made the Fool, and Geoffrey did not know exactly what forces had. Something French, he imagined, which was to say something incomprehensible. Something men decided to make of themselves. Was there, he wondered, a guild of Fools? Did God measure such behavior a kind of penance? Of course not, thought Geoffrey, trailing one hand along the cold stone of the corridor. And if the Fool took pleasure in such behavior, wasn't it a bit like sinfulness? The wrinkled priest who had instructed Geoffrey as a boy had been gentle but sure-handed. ''But Christ's mercy, and Mary and John, these are the ground of all my bliss," the priest had said, smiling in a tired way, as if such bliss wore out the very soul it claimed. Plainly any bliss not grounded in Christ was grounded in something potentially wicked.

He slipped into the East Tower and froze at the sight of a candle, a stab of light in the blackness. He put a hand on a manuscript and whispered, "Good evening," a neutral greeting he would use with anyone, because he had expected darkness.

A shadow spilled across a wall. An arm, cast in gold in the light of the candle, and the curve of a woman's hip beneath gray cloth. "My lord?"

Someday, thought Geoffrey, I will change my life. Someday—when I am a stronger, better man.

"My lord," she repeated, knowing in every gesture, the shaking down of her dark hair, the hook of her thumb into a fold of his tunic, that he had admired more than her voice. She drew him into the candlelight. The candle was a stub, smoking, the scent of servants' wax.

Rain. A clatter of hoofbeats, unimportant, far away. The candle sizzled, and the light wavered for a moment, like the shadow of someone passing across the room. The floor was hard.

More hoofbeats, an unusual number, he realized vaguely. The distant voice of a guard, words indistinct.

The grind of doors thrown open, the squeal of window shutters swung wide. The jabber of many voices. Voices he knew well. Very well. The sheriff sat up.

Baldwin!

Henry still could not speak and gestured: please wait.

"You really should eat less, Henry," Geoffrey snapped.

Henry held forth his hands, pleading, and gasped, "My lord, Baldwin has returned."

"Why?"

"The problem is worse than we thought, my lord—"

Geoffrey flung Henry to one side and ran into the great hall.

Baldwin shoved chairs out of his way, pacing, his white hair soaked and sticking up in bristles all over his head. "Geoffrey, for all my love of you I won't be able to spare the king this ghastly news."

"My dear Baldwin, you're soaked."

"And I myself will never forgive what has happened as long as I live. On the King's High Way, to a very steward to the king."

"We will have some wine . . ." Geoffrey began.

"Wine! God's piss, we will have blood," Baldwin thundered. "Not half a day out of Nottingham, south on the king's road, that highwayman and his rat-faced gang waylay us, capture us, force us to attend a feast tied like calves, and let us go only this afternoon after having full sport with us. Demonstrating their skill with sword, stave, and arrow, as if we were a happy audience. The man is a very devil, Geoffrey, a very filthy, corrupt, and criminal devil."

"You spent the night in the forest?"

"Yes! And he laughed constantly. Forever laughing, as if the entire episode, every passing wet minute of it, were a joke, a sport, an amusement for himself and his tattered fellows."

"How many dead?" asked Geoffrey grimly.

"What?"

"How many of your party are—"

"No one. None of us is hurt. It's the fact of it. The fact, Geoffrey. The mockery of it. He held, and I am a Christian, a mock court, a mock feast table, a mock fire, as if flame could share in a prank, snapping and sparking like laughter, at me, Geoffrey! At the king, Geoffrey, and at you! I'm afraid, Geoffrey, and forgive me. Forgive me, I beg, but I fear that you have more than met your match."

"I have a plan, Baldwin."

Baldwin stared into his wine cup as if it contained human brains. "We don't need plans, Geoffrey, although I know they are your great strength. By Jesus' face, we need results."

"You talk as if a man of action were required. One of those sword wielders from Byzantium. And then you change your tune and describe an outlaw only a subtle man can catch. I am your subtle man."

Baldwin sighed. "Pray God you're right."

Geoffrey beckoned. Henry clumped across the floor and stood, still red-cheeked.

"Declare the following regarding this man," said Geoffrey. "He is now legally, and not simply in effect, an outlaw. Any man who finds him can kill him with impunity. The law offers him nothing, not mercy, not recognition of name or status, nor does it see him as a child under the roof of the king's power. It is as if he were not born.''

Henry bowed. It was no easy thing, condemning a man. Henry marched into the darkness that surrounded them, a man carrying out a death warrant.

Geoffrey sat heavily. The command had taken the last fire out of him. ''Don't worry for even a moment, Baldwin. I will net this man, and every man with him, because to catch one fly is nothing. I will catch them all. With a trick. What is a net but a thing which seems not to be there, by being mostly space? I will seem powerless. I will seem to be asleep, unconcerned. Like a spider, I will feel everything. I will hide just out of sight, an eye filled with poison. Because I know games. I know the game between men and women, between torturer and prisoner, and between hunter and quarry. Tell the king that his spider is awake and waiting.''

15

hugh wished Henry a good morning.

Henry nodded, too preoccupied to speak. Sometimes Hugh envied Henry. Henry tried hard, took a hitch at his sword belt before he spoke, but Hugh had the feeling that Henry was not quite equal to the challenges God set before him. Nevertheless, Henry was entrusted with the forest work, leading spearmen on horseback.

Hugh had put any scandal regarding the sheriff, and any disappointment he might have felt towards the sheriff, out of his mind. He hurried to bring the sheriff a knife for his goose quill and shifted the leaden lion's head paperweight so it pressed the vellum at the right-hand corner where it curled.

Hugh was gratified at the smile Geoffrey gave him. He could not help noticing that when the sheriff spoke to Henry, a frown line appeared between the sheriff's eyebrows.

It was necessary to sign a written edict declaring Robin Hood an outlaw; his spoken declaration to Henry had been impressive but not entirely lawful. The condition of outlawry had in years past stripped a man of all protection of the law. It had been a form of banishment, and such a man's life had been virtually forfeit. The law was changing, much the way an oak changes its outline over decades, casting a greater shadow, more impressive, more protective. Now a pronouncement of outlawry meant that the man should be apprehended and brought to trial. Naturally, if he were killed in the process, no great harm would have been done.

The goose quill plunged into the pot of black. Geoffrey wrote his name, the jagged letters staggering across the bottom of the parchment, the quill squeaking, the ink floating in the final *y*, almost spilling over the confines of the letter, but settling at last.

"Government is composed of documents," said Geoffrey. "They are the skeleton of law."

Henry grunted agreement, but what did Henry know? He dreamed of the future when his own name was scrawled at the bottom of such sheets of vellum, in those years after Geoffrey had doddered into retirement and Henry had learned to write.

Deliberately Geoffrey dipped the fingernail-pale quill deeper into black. He tapped the quill against the inkpot, and a single drop of black extended itself and fell. He wrote, after his name, "Scyrreve of Notyngham," and blew on the words as they dimmed from brilliant newness to dull permanence.

As always when he had either read or written, Geoffrey felt that something had been accomplished. Events were messy. Deer slipped, struggled, and were torn to sloppy bits by hounds. Words and numbers lasted, iron hooks of reality a man could cling to and be certain. Seasons changed, summer calcifying into winter, but the prayers learned in childhood followed the soul, like stitches in a hem.

Baldwin and his men left at dawn, the sky rust brown where the sun bled through the clouds. Geoffrey stood on the walls and watched the king's men ride through the streets, chasing a single gray cat until it darted behind a drain barrel. He waited until he could see the horsemen in the distance, a smudge of men and horses on the High Way.

In the other direction was the event he had deliberately avoided. A figure hung from the gibbet, and a small group of men returned to the city, beyond the peaked roofs and chimney smoke. Already a black bird fell across the sky like a single hard coal and circled the stout beams of wood.

"So," said Geoffrey, "whatever he buried will remain in the earth."

Hugh fastened Geoffrey's cape against a gust of wind.

"By law I have to ride out to the gibbet. To make sure that the right body hangs there. I can't say it is one of my favorite duties. You come, too. I know you've seen men hanged before. But you don't know what it is to have done it yourself. Oh, Nottingham did the deed. But he was my agent, a pair of hands I ordered forth to do what my station would not allow me to commit myself. I killed him." Geoffrey smiled a thin smile. "I had no choice. My mercy struck the man as cruel."

Hugh made the expression of one who understood every word.

It began to rain as they rode through the streets. The same cat lunged and paused, then hid again as they began to gallop. Rain kissed Geoffrey's eyes, and he hunched down into the horse's mane.

A lifetime among horses, the smell of them, straw and hay, and the pepper of manure on cold mornings, as if the wind itself were fertile. The creak of leather, the jangle of the bridles, decorated with fringe and buttons, brass polished until it gleamed and fired the sun back into the sky in dozens of fragments. And war-horses, with armor covering their nostrils and high-fronted saddles so a man could lean forwards to the kill without pitching off the horse, the pommel a bulwark against gut wounds. Geoffrey had trained until almost any horse knew immediately what he wanted, even the most muscular battle-stallion.

The horse he rode now was a gray war-horse, without armor. A simple red rope was the bridle, and a plain brass bit matched the brass stirrup. The rain made patches of the horse's hair stand up, like grass a dog has been playing in, and when the horse tossed its mane, water flew into the air. They rode the long way round, to delay their arrival at the gibbet.

The mill wheel turned with a ground-shivering rumble as the stones inside the mill itself turned. The miller squinted up at them as they passed, acknowledging unthinkingly the natural superiority of a mounted man compared with a man on foot. The miller had wide black nostrils and was powdered with white. Rain streaked the flour as he waved to the sheriff, a wave that was necessary; a man had to be respectful to the king's law. Still, within the confines of manners and common sense, it was possible to show some disdain for order. The miller, like so many millers, wanted more than God had allotted him.

Geoffrey made a point of stopping. "Good day to you, miller."

"Good enough, for wet," said the miller, showing three brown teeth. A bagpipe lay in a heap on the floor behind him, and a stave leaned against the wall. Those music-making bladders were popular among unpleasant people. "My son is very pleased with you, I must report."

"I am honored," said Geoffrey.

"He's entering the tournament."

"Tournament?"

"The archery." Not "The archery, sire," an obnoxious lack of manners that was, of course, deliberate.

"I look forward to seeing his shooting."

"He'll split the prick five times out of six and none better."

"That's very impressive."

"They hanged a thief today," said the miller.

Geoffrey allowed himself a smile. "I know that," he said.

"But it won't do any good. Men who steal know they

86

take their lives in their hands. They decide to be dead men and feed their families.''

How charmless men became when they decided to be outspoken. "I had always thought of greed as a sin," said Geoffrey.

"And so God will punish in His good time. But what can folk do when God Himself makes hungry children?"

"If your son shoots as well as his father talks, he will win the mark indeed."

"There's a certain freedom to an outlaw," said the miller.

Geoffrey made a dry laugh. "And this from you. No man is less an outlaw than a miller. You drudge, joined to your place by the river, to your millstones, to your space on the earth."

The miller made a brown smile.

"The law is a miller's friend," Geoffrey concluded.

"And the outlaw's, too. An outlaw knows he may be dead tomorrow, and he can fling himself away with a laugh, because what choice does he have?"

"Your mother was an argumentative soul, as I recall," said Geoffrey, smiling.

The miller's face tightened.

"She'd argue with a water trough as soon as pass it," said Geoffrey merrily.

The miller twisted his face into a grin. "She had a tongue. And she raised a son with an eye in his head to see what's taking place round him. The word is, my lord—"

The sudden courtesy cut Geoffrey, and he tightened his hold on the reins.

The miller came close and put a floury hand out to Geoffrey's knee. "The word is, my lord, that while you have spent time with the ladies, forgive me, sire, Robin Hood has been visiting the city streets, under your very nose."

"That prankster? I know he has been doing such things, and I realize he finds it humorous," Geoffrey lied. "And I have been allowing him this freedom, as a man might allow a puppy to get well into mischief before cutting a switch, especially if the man has weighty matters on hand. His time has run out, but I don't have the desire at this point to beat him yet. You may say I enjoy the company of ladies, or you may say I am closeted with my accounts. At any rate, I am too—"

"Certain ladies, they say, sire. Certain ladies who, speaking properly, have no business even looking at a man. At even casting an eye in the direction of his finger." The word *finger* was enunciated with elaborate care. "A certain particular lady who has no such business, and I beg my lord's pardon."

"I am too busy to bother with the prankster, except to declare him outlaw. I will get to him in my own good time. As for the gossip you have gathered under your nails, I have seen several tongues cut out in my day and have always marveled at the transformation it makes in a man."

A slow smile, with three brown teeth, and the miller's eyes disappeared with merriment. "Well said, sire. These tinkers who wander from place to place have so little better to talk about, you might as well cut off

tongue, nose, cock, toes, and leave them but one eye
while you're about it."

"SUCH A DREADFUL MAN," said Hugh when they had
left the miller behind them.

"What? Oh, him. He simply gave me something to
think on."

The thief's eyes were half open. Geoffrey saw that
much and looked away.

"I wanted to strike the man down," said Hugh.

"The miller? He is a man who is afraid of the law
inside himself. And to prove otherwise to himself, he
acts as obnoxious as possible in the face of it. Why do
we have to worry ourselves over men like him when we
have the power to do this to a thief?"

Hugh had seen many men hanged, and he gazed at
the bare feet of the figure on the gibbet. A carrion crow
soared over the cross-beam, fluttered, and landed at the
rope wound round the span of wood.

Sheep crowded the hillside, the color of maggots, and
the stink of them perfumed the wind. Not one lifted its
head. A shepherd leaned on his staff, staring at the
backs of the sheep that surrounded him. He wore a
cloak that wrapped him and a cap that gave his head
the shape of a thumb.

They rode until they reached the High Way. Baldwin's
men had destroyed the rain-smoothed surface of the
mud. Many of the hoofprints were gray with rainwater,
but it was not raining now. Faint blue shifted across

the sky, and the clouds yellowed where the sun broke overhead.

The High Way was a simple stretch of mud. The King's Forest crowded either side, saplings along the edge where the older trees had been cleared. The green-black trees were a physical manifestation of the majesty of the law. Birds fluttered from branch to ground, unaware they were supported by justice just as a man's hand is stayed or freed by the hand of God. Geoffrey did not know why, but he was at peace. At peace, in the midst of these terrible burdens.

But just as an outlaw was freed by being condemned, so a man of law was freed by having so much responsibility he had no freedom at all. He need not decide what to do next. He had no choice but to do exactly what was required of him.

16

The market was rich with food, some still struggling. Chickens in wooden cages fluttered and stared. A feather floated like a star in the air. A goose, tied by a rope to a pole, had collapsed. It lunged feebly at a laughing boy and was too tired to do more than hiss. Pickerel and carp glittered in baskets, and there were bunches of watercress. A pile of cabbages hulked beside wheels of white cheeses. A basket shivered, and a bird worked its head through the lid and beheld the market with a copper-bright eye. A broad hand shoved the bird back where it belonged, and a voice called, "Pee-jons!"

Bunches of parsnips gleamed under the mud that smeared them. Great domes of black bread glistened in the sun. Turnips with purple markings like bruises tumbled onto a blanket. Everywhere the air was noisy with haggling, and laughter, and gossip. Respectful heads bowed as Geoffrey passed, and he declined offers of an apple, a wedge of bread, and a slab of cheese mottled and gleaming like a cornerstone.

But summer was over. The last of the fat harvest was in, and already the carrots were huge bulbs, distended with too much growth, like goiters, or thin and overlong, tapering to long white hairs. Barley had been transformed to barrels of ale, and the lambs that bleated and tugged against ropes were already too leggy to fetch the highest price. Even the cabbage was tinged with brown, the slowest-selling or slowest-growing heads already turning their outer leaves into skulls within which the brains were shrinking.

"WHAT DID YOU DO with this sword, sire?" asked Ivo. "What caused it to be like this, if I may ask?"

"I attacked a plant. I believe it was a holly bush."

Ivo squinted along the blade, letting his eye slowly open when it met Geoffrey's gaze. "A holly bush?"

"I was very angry."

"But you don't want to do that sort of thing, now do you, my lord?"

"Not as a rule."

"Ever," Ivo snapped. "Forgive me, I value steel above everything. My father was a furbisher, as was my grandfather, and we all loved steel more than meat, more than women, nearly."

"I understand," said Geoffrey.

Ivo laid the sword gently on a bench that was hacked and scarred. He ran a finger along the flat of another blade. "To see a blemish in a perfect thing pains me. A blemish implies fragility, as in a man it implies sin."

"Naturally."

"Sin in a sword snaps it. Now, you can fight with a snapped sword. Sir Roger gutted a Saracen with a sword like a shard of glass. I was there—surrounded by Damascus steel, our English blade irons dragging our arms weak. Sir Roger's blade rang sour, like a piss-pot struck with a spoon, and the thing shattered. Upright, like a finger of glass, and the infidel, with his victory in his teeth, before he could grin, was fed his own bowels. Quick Sir Roger! Such a sight! He took that broken steel as you'd take a finger into butter and slipped it from cock to breast before you'd blink."

Ivo patted the sword and found a purple-stained rag. "Not, however, the best way to slit a man, Christian or not. So, and forgive me, when you bring me a weapon of fine steel, smooth as cream, not even the tiniest of flaws, all gory with tree sap, I am"—Ivo cranked his vise, a noise like a bird's chirp—"I am angry." He made the word long: "ang-gry."

He rubbed the blade with a tincture that smelled like vinegar. "Although, forgive me. No doubt the holly bush offended the king's man in some manner not understood by a lowly furbisher."

Geoffrey's fondness for Ivo was insufficient antidote for his irritation. "I have many worries, Ivo. Sometimes I can't control my anger."

"It's balance you need, not control, and forgive my brazen mouth. Too much spleen, and you need soak it up! Spleen-stone! Ask the surgeon—he has cured my foul humors many times with a little rock, a little green-ish serpentine, my lord.''

The furbisher squinted along the blade, then sat and pedaled his wheel. The whetstone sang, and the sword spit sparks. ''The finest edge can be made crooked by hacking the most common wood. Just the way the smart-est man can be made a little stupid by the commonest wine.''

''Will your son be in the tournament?''

''Or lose both arms!''

''He must be practicing now.''

''That's why he's not here. He's bending a bow out with dozens of the same mind.''

''Good luck to him.''

Ivo cradled the sword in his hands. ''And good luck to you with this sword, my lord. And thank you for your patience with a simpleton's chatter.''

The sun in the courtyard was warm, and the shadow too cool. Icy hands of darkness closed round Geoffrey in the chapel as he waited for his eyes to adjust.

A segment of glass had fallen from a chapel window, a section of sky above an angel. Geoffrey picked up the triangle of sky, brittle as a wafer and miraculously unbroken.

The colored glass of this chapel was perhaps the most beautiful thing in the shire. It showed residents of Heaven, angels dressed in gowns that flowed to their ankles. They wore simple belts round their waists, except for the Archangel Michael, who was armored and car-ried a sword. The other angels carried trumpets or staffs and seemed ready to drop even those simple objects and take flight. When they gestured, the sleeves of their gowns fell back to expose graceful forearms. Their halos set off their heads not only from their bodies but from everything else in the window, from the chapel, even from the other angels. Each angel was complete in his own bubble, circumscribed by his own holiness.

Geoffrey held the segment of glass Heaven in his hand as he prayed to the Queen of Courtesy, who knew every flaw that made him fragile. On his way out he stopped to gaze upwards through the wound in the window, through which actual day, bright and colorless, was shining. Through that hole in the perfection the sounds of the world outside were bleeding: the chime of the blacksmith's hammer, the rumble of a wagon. The angels, surrounded by their own magnificence, noticed neither the profane murmur from outside nor the uplifted eyes of the sinner before them.

Hugh stood in the soft, multicolored light. Waiting, a young man with the frame and steady eye of a warrior but with a youth's shyness. "Sometimes our own character is imperfect," Geoffrey heard himself say.

"Indeed, my lord," said Hugh.

Why, Geoffrey wondered, does this brief response make me feel so desolate?

"But like a gap in a window, perhaps a man's character can be healed." Hugh pressed his lips tight, perhaps embarrassed by this flower of speech.

An ill feeling that had flourished in Geoffrey died, a weed of self-hatred. He almost confided in Hugh at that moment. He almost said, Do you think we can outwit Robin Hood?

17

Too many archers thought they were superior to any man who had ever drawn a bow, and too many men failed to split the prick, a small black wand in the center of the target. At one hundred paces it was difficult but by no means impossible, as Geoffrey explained to Sir Roger, who squinted across the green towards the butts with an expression of disgust.

The weak ones would be weeded out, Geoffrey explained, by this series of eliminations, until by the time the last four faced the targets they would see the sort of shooting a man could imagine taking place only in Heaven.

Lady Eleanor kept well under the canopy, whispering to her lady-in-waiting, the same furtive creature who acted as her chambermaid, and they both giggled. No doubt the sight of so many well-stockinged men exhilarated them.

"Who is that?" Geoffrey whispered to Hugh, who stood beside him.

"Thurstin, son of the miller. Strong-looking, but I doubt a miller's son can compete with the foresters."

The arrows struck the target with a smack, like the flat of a sword striking wood. A cry signaled a good shot, then a groan indicated a miss, as the archers stepped up and took their turns, reacting or remaining calm, as fitted their temperaments. The sky was clear blue, and the grass perfect green. Peddlers offered hens on skewers, and beggars, driven off by the sheriff's men with black pikes, worked the edge of the crowd, shuffling and stooping as their state required.

Geoffrey could speak lightly, but it was obvious that the highwayman had not come to the tournament, and a terrible taste rose within him: the realization that this trap had failed. The sight of his wife leaving the tournament did nothing to cheer him. "The sight of your beauty would encourage many a fine archer," Geoffrey said.

"I am afraid that I am not well," she said. "I have a headache, and now, furthermore, I have a heaviness in my stomach." She said this with a soft voice and a sideways glance that implied that Geoffrey had caused her to be ill.

"I wonder why there is a crowd of people around that potter's cart," Geoffrey said idly.

"Perhaps the pots are of unusual quality."

"How can a pot be of unusual quality?"

"There are excellent pots, and not excellent ones, too."

"I have never given it much thought."

"I have, and I shall send my maid to see what excites these people," said Eleanor tartly.

Geoffrey smiled and nodded to a passing franklin. "You do this simply to annoy me. You have no more interest in pots than you do in oxtails."

"Most marvelous pots," the maid panted upon her return. "And a most witty potter, who says that my lady could have the entire cart for three pennies."

"The man is a simpleton," said Geoffrey.

THE DOCTOR WAITED with a great show of patience, a careful smile on his lips, his hands clasped, demonstrating that wisdom gave a man peace and that the more he was forced to endure the outrageousness of the world, the more patient he would become. He was dressed in blue, with a blue cap that flowed down his back and blue inner sleeves, to show that Heaven itself had charged him with wisdom.

"What is wrong with my wife?" asked Geoffrey. It was late afternoon, the castle quiet after the pageantry of the tournament.

"She has a phlegmatic stomach," said the doctor with a smile.

"Can it be cured?"

The doctor smiled as if delighted. "It can be cured, with time and with the proper ministrations of the correct foods and herbs."

"What have you done for her anxiety?"

"Anxiety is easily cured. The nerves are the simplest

aspect of the body to act upon. I have given her a potion made from sage."

"And what is that?" asked Geoffrey.

"An herb that grows in the sun in countries of the south and, since it absorbs the sun, delivers its influence into the body. It does have one danger, which is—my lord, don't worry; I have never seen such a solicitous husband—that it removes the dark color from the hair. But it is simple to add to the potion a tincture of myrtle and garden crocus, and then there is no danger whatso-ever."

"I am glad I talked with you, Doctor. I am much reassured."

"You seem much disturbed yourself, my lord."

"I have concerns, but I am well enough."

"Allow me to prescribe a mash of rye. It breaks down the concentration of humors."

Geoffrey started. "You think there's something wrong?"

"A precaution, my lord. Simply a precaution. And yet—" The doctor reached forth his slender hands, and Geoffrey cringed before he managed to hold himself still. The physician peered into Geoffrey's eyes, pulling the lower lids down. "And yet I do see some cause for concern. Your blood may be too cold."

"Too cold?"

"Mmm. Yes, I fear so. Easily remedied, however, my lord."

"Is it serious?"

"Unchecked, yes, it could well be. Any imbalance, my lord, is undesirable. What we seek is a balance between the four humors, between warmth and coolness, between passion and wisdom, a perfect harmony. Not too much passion, not too much thought, not too much wind, not too much staleness of air. In short, we desire that the elaborate ship of the body be entirely well balanced so that it tips not too much in one direction or another."

"What can I do?"

"I will prescribe wheat soup. It irritates the respiratory passages, but that effect is neutralized by mixing it with warm water."

"This will cure me?"

"There can be no doubt, my lord."

Geoffrey stepped close and murmured, "There is one further trouble, my dear doctor, which I am reluctant to confess."

"I am at your service, my lord."

"My nature has always been passionate," Geoffrey began. "This passion has been a cause of grief to me. I am, to be brief, overly lustful. Although any lust at all is grievous." Geoffrey faltered.

The physician closed his eyes and lifted a hand. "Have no fear, my lord. I understand perfectly. You are filled with an understandable desire for your wife's affections and yet do not want to trouble her during her illness."

"Exactly."

"I know of an excellent medicine for the damping of the desire for coitus. Furthermore, it sharpens the eyesight and dissipates flatulence."

"What is it?"

"Rue. I have some of the optimum variety, that which was grown near a fig tree."

Geoffrey shook the vial in his hand, studying the grainy brown surface of the clay. The cork worked free with a wet pop. "I can't see into it."

"Two good, strong gulps would start the cure, and then just before sleep tonight you should finish the rest, because it is at night that desire is at its apex."

Geoffrey swallowed, once, twice.

"Jesus' Face, that's the bitterest stuff I've ever tasted in my life!"

"No good is accomplished without travail," said the physician.

18

I am very pleased with the quality of these pots," said Lady Eleanor that evening. "I am very sorry that you have only five left."

"The sorrow is all mine, my lady. But when the people heard me calling 'Pots, cheap!' they came running."

Geoffrey eyed the potter without much interest, carving the rind off a green apple. The man was dressed in tatters, but his shoes were of good quality, the sort a footman might wear while accompanying a hunt, and the sword at his side was in a black scabbard tipped with brass.

"Why," asked Geoffrey, "did you sell so cheap?"

"I wanted to enter into the spirit of the tournament. What better way than to sell everything as cheaply as possible? And now, my lord, I am so sorry to have sold all but five, I give these to you as a gift, from my heart."

"Oh, no!" said Lady Eleanor, looking pink-cheeked and alert. "Allow us to compensate you for your skill and for your—"

"We are grateful, and we accept your gift," said Geoffrey. The apple was now bare of skin. He cut the fruit in two and dug the pits out with the point of the paring knife. "You do not come from this shire, do you, potter?"

"No, my lord, and it's difficult to say where exactly I do come from. I travel so much plying my trade that I seem to be everywhere at once."

"How marvelous it must be to be everywhere at once," laughed Lady Eleanor. "Sometimes I feel that I am nowhere at all."

"And that, my lady, must be a terrible sensation."

"Oh, it is, my good potter, it is indeed. But you will allow us to provide you with a meal. You will dine with us, potter."

"By all means," said Geoffrey with no enthusiasm. "You will join us and tell us stories of the road."

It was not unheard of for the sheriff to entertain a traveler, such as a minstrel or a wayfaring merchant. A potter was a lowly guest, but this potter did have a gentle, courteous voice and a way about him that was immediately appealing, an eagerness to have fellowship that inspired even Eleanor. Geoffrey chewed his apple and hoped, dimly, that the potter would provide diverting conversation. It was not a strong hope and faded as he realized that Eleanor was more interested in the man's leg, and in the man's quick eye and merry laugh, than in his conversation.

The potter wore a borrowed tunic to the table, a coarse wool equal to a wealthy miller or a traveling clerk from a distant shire come to give the compliments of his own sheriff. The potter drank deep of the slightly inferior white wine the sheriff served tonight, and the candlelight made the craftsman's face dance with shadows and made his eyes twinkle above his auburn beard.

Geoffrey sucked the flesh off a partridge's wing and leaned forwards. "You are from north of here, I gather."

"True enough, my lord. From north of here, but not far."

"From where, exactly, if you will forgive my being blunt?"

"My lord, you must be blunt. A sheriff has many duties and many worries on his mind. A humble potter can talk, chattering like a finch in the bush, all day, and no one will mark a single word."

"My husband was born blunt. If he were a potter, he would sell every pot for as much as he could, walk all over the shire with a full cart as a consequence, and die of weariness." She picked at the leg of a bird, but apparently the physician's potions had not yet helped her stomach.

"Where?" asked Geoffrey calmly, as if all intervening talk had been the merest rustling of leaves.

"Barnsdale, my lord."

"You carry a sword."

"These days even millers carry swords, and bucklers, too. I have to protect myself from envious potters, who lack skill and business sense."

"You pushed your cart through Sherwood Forest?"

"With these stout arms."

The potter held up one arm, letting the sleeve of the coarse tunic fall, and displayed a muscular arm, and brown, too, from the sun.

"And no one troubled you along the way?"

"No one. Save a surly miller who swore that traveling craftsmen should be strung from a gibbet."

"One of our local gentlefolk," Geoffrey said. "He is worse than the sourest of women when it comes to saying the exact words a man doesn't want to hear. And yet I understand that his son, Thurstin, won the gold mark today."

"A worthy accomplishment."

"Especially when you consider that we have, here in Nottingham, the finest archers in the kingdom."

"I see you have a Fool, my lord."

"Yes."

"Isn't he the wittiest creature? See! He chews exactly like my husband."

Geoffrey spoke with more lightness than he felt. "My wife enjoys him, and guests find him amusing."

"But the credit is yours, my lord."

"How mine?"

"For allowing yourself to be mocked in your own household. This is a mark of greatness and subtlety. You allow others their laugh and attain thereby a greater stature."

Geoffrey nodded in acknowledgment of the flattery, but he was struck by the potter's vocabulary. *Subtlety* was the sort of word Baldwin understood, a word that itself required subtlety, if not a court background. And yet the potter planted his elbows on the table and chewed with the unconcern of a wandering craftsman. "I am not as pleased as you think me to be," said Geoffrey. "I tolerate him."

"Just as you tolerate flattery from your inferiors, my lord."

"I am told that you are a skilled potter."

"I have studied my craft."

"Was your father a potter?"

"And his father, off into the past. All of us potters, clay between our fingers spun by the kicking wheel."

"And have you always plied your wares on the road?"

"No, I have only recently begun to travel. I heard of the great prosperity of Nottingham under the guidance of the sheriff, and I knew I had to travel here, pushing my wares ahead of me. A dull way to travel. You see constantly exactly what is ahead of you, exactly what you saw at home: rows of pots."

"Your hands are not callused in the places a cart pusher's hands are callused, and you are too light of step to be a man who has done it long."

"They told me, and I did not believe it. They said, and I did not hear. The sheriff of Nottingham is canny. That's what they said. He sees and he knows. Sees and knows. That's what they said."

Geoffrey wiped his mouth. "If you wanted to make money, why did you stand calling out that you were practically giving your pots away and proceed to do exactly that?"

"A cartload of pots is a heavy thing, my lord."

Geoffrey regretted the cheap wine. A servingman in

drab gray livery poured Geoffrey some more, and Geoffrey sat back to watch the Fool, who was juggling four red wooden balls, to the delight of Lady Eleanor.

"What brought you to Nottingham today, potter?"

"The tournament, my lord."

"It was a wonderful sight, and you missed it by selling your pots."

"I came not to watch it, my lord, but to participate."

"And you came too late."

"To my great sorrow, my lord. And yet not too late to challenge the winner."

Geoffrey sipped the wine. "You love games, potter?"

"They are my passion."

Geoffrey crooked a finger and said to a servant, "Bring us some bows." For a moment the sheriff said nothing. "What sort of contest do you suggest?" he asked at last, as if he cared little.

"Nothing unusual. A simple feat of archery. Say, an arrow sunk into a roof beam in the great hall, and that arrow split, and that one split, until a last, tenth arrow stands where the others stood. And I put this ounce of gold down as a wager that I can best the miller's son."

The servant brought bows, and the potter stood and selected one. He flexed it, then, with one fluid motion, strung the bow and held it at arm's length. "This," said the potter, "is right weak gear."

Geoffrey made a gesture of apology.

"But I have in my cart outside another bow, a bow that Robin Hood gave me."

Geoffrey gently put down his wine cup and leaned forwards. "You know Robin Hood?" he asked softly.

"Know him! Many times Robin Hood and I have shot under the Trysting Oak."

"Go and get your bow," said the sheriff.

The man left, and Geoffrey watched the Fool balance a chair on his chin, his nimble feet moving constantly. Geoffrey touched the arm of a servant and ordered that the miller's son be sent for. And then he sat back, at peace for the first time in days. It was the peace that rises within a man in the midst of danger, like water welling from a spring.

Geoffrey closed his eyes. The Fool's feet whispered on the stone floor. The whippet scratched itself, the nails of its foot making rhythmic strokes against its hide. Eleanor clapped her hands at yet another of the Fool's stunts.

19

ugh looked on, aware of the sputter of each candle, the hiss of the man-sized logs in the fireplace. The potter held a special fascination for Hugh, as he did for the sheriff. The sheriff's eyes followed the potter, every movement he made, ignoring Thurstin.

The great hall was too dark, and torches were brought, spitting and smoking, gilding the men with half-light.

"This," said the potter, "is the bow given to me by Robin Hood himself."

"Robin Hood!" breathed Thurstin, holding forth his hand to touch the blond span of wood.

"Its length suits you well," said the sheriff.

"It's a good bow," said the potter easily, as if such things did not matter much to him.

High above them windows creaked in a gust of wind, and needles of water glinted in the torchlight. "I am glad the skies were blue for today's contest," said the sheriff. "Like so much in life, weather can change suddenly for the worse."

"Or for the better," said the potter.

"This is true," said Geoffrey. "Although pleasant surprises do not usually concern us."

Thurstin said nothing, his eyes alight.

The potter gestured towards the cross-beam, high above them in the shifting torchlight. "My lord sheriff, plant an arrow in that beam as a target."

"The bow is not one of my skills," said Geoffrey.

"Nor should it be," said the potter. "A gentleman's weapon is his sword."

"Or his tongue," said the sheriff.

Quickly, with a fluid motion so sudden as to be nearly invisible, the potter strung his bow, selected a pale shaft, planted a foot, and sent an arrow into the beam above them. The arrow shivered, deep into the wood, and the sound of it echoed in the hall like the bite of an axe.

Thurstin whistled softly.

"So," said Geoffrey, recovering himself. "Thurstin, try to split this arrow prick with ten shots. I will back this good miller's son with a wager of my own."

The potter's smile gleamed in the torchlight.

Thurstin strung his bow with a grunt and sorted through the arrows on the table.

"My arrows, I think, are better," said the potter.

"Much," said Thurstin. The young man flexed his bow, nocked the arrow, and drew it to his ear.

The arrow missed by a hand's breadth and bounded off the hard wood of the beam, clattering to the floor.

"The light here is very bad," said the sheriff.

"The light is good enough," said Thurstin disgustedly. He plucked another arrow and took a deep breath.

Another miss, although by less than a hand, and the arrow stuck.

"A good shot," said the potter.

Thurstin made a thin-lipped smile and selected another arrow. This arrow trembled in the beam no closer to the target arrow, but deeper into the wood.

"Good!" said Geoffrey, and it was good, shooting upwards like that, in the shivering torch shadows. The miller's son was a credit to the city.

Again and again, until ten arrows had been sent, all of them missing the target arrow, but the last quivering in the beam so close to the target arrow the two looked intertwined.

"Excellent!" said the sheriff.

"A good eye and a steady hand," said the potter.

Thurstin shrugged and unstrung his bow. "I could do worse," he said.

"Indeed much worse," said the sheriff. "And now, our guest."

The potter inclined his head in a brief bow.

"Plant another target arrow," said the sheriff. "Off to one side.

As if planted in the beam by thought alone, another arrow buried itself into the roof beam, and this arrow did not quiver, sunk so far into the wood that it was like a part of the timber, a straight black twig out of the heart of the wood itself.

The potter counted ten arrows and tucked them into

his belt. He moved in an unhurried manner. When the arrows were tucked through his belt, and he stood in the same place Thurstin had stood, the potter took a long moment to listen, it seemed, to the rain.

The potter took a step to the side and held his bow loosely in his fingers, the way the angels in the window held their trumpets, ready to play or to abandon their instruments and fly.

Geoffrey jumped at the noise. The chunk of the arrow, and the high, splintered shower of arrow on the stone floor. A single shaft stood out from the timber, casting a black shadow.

It seemed a mistake, and by the time Geoffrey understood what had happened, nine more arrows had buried themselves into the cross-beam with a sound like axe-heads buried into wood, and all but the last arrow had showered, splintered, to the floor.

Torches whispered. Silently the potter unstrung his bow. "I am sorry," he said softly, "that I was late for the tournament."

"And I, too," said Geoffrey, when he could speak, "am sorry." He felt into his tunic. "But you have won this gold honorably."

The coins disappeared as the potter's hand closed round them. "You shot well," said the potter.

Thurstin threw his bow to the table. "Well!"

"I have had practice."

"You got this bow from Robin Hood?" asked the sheriff.

The potter stirred himself, as if from deep thought. "Yes, from the man himself."

"I have long wanted to meet this man Robin Hood."

"A thing easily done. He meets many people and without their even asking. I am sure that if a man asks to see him, it will be all the more easy."

The amazing feat seemed to have taken the fire out of the potter. He sat and said softly, "Come with me tomorrow—alone. I will take you to Robin Hood."

"Where does he live?" asked Geoffrey lightly, although inside he was trembling.

"In the greenwood."

"The greenwood surrounds us."

"He will meet you there."

"You seem certain of this."

The potter met the sheriff's gaze, and the torchlight glittered in the potter's smile and in his eyes, and the man said, "There can be no doubt."

Geoffrey could not think, calmed strangely by the man's smile. "Spend the night here, then, and we will leave tomorrow to see Robin Hood."

Hugh stood beside the newel-post of the stairs, holding his breath. There was the slightest hope that the sheriff would turn with a smile and say, Hugh, you can come, too.

Hugh, I can't ride into the forest without you.

But he didn't.

20

Hugh dreamed that he was alone in the forest, screeching ravens overhead. Each shadow of each tree fell across his running body, a shaft of cold. Hugh woke shivering, thankful that he was on his duck-feather pallet, within the walls of the castle.

A worthy plan was in place: Henry was to follow secretly, trailing the sheriff. But Hugh was uneasy.

As he fastened the sheriff's iron spurs the following morning, Hugh heard himself wish the sheriff well. "Saint Christopher protect you, my lord," he said. These were not mere house spurs. These were black iron vises, ending with a star-shaped rowel, not the usual arrowpoint, an innovation that would permit a stroke instead of a stab; the Alsatians had invented them.

Don't go, Hugh wanted to warn the sheriff. *Stay here.*

THE POTTER CLIMBED onto the back of a gray gelding like a man who knew horses but who had not ridden in a long while. His feet found the simple iron stirrups with difficulty, and he reined too hard, working the iron bit into the horse's mouth. But he calmed the horse easily, with a touch and a low word, and smiled into the morning sun. "I thank you for loaning me this mount," he said. "It is another example of your generosity to a stranger."

Geoffrey kept the bright sun behind his left shoulder as he studied the potter. The man was as tanned as a peasant, and muscular, and the sun glinted off his russet beard. He wore his bow across his back, the string across the front of his loose, ragged tunic. The two men studied each other, but Geoffrey allowed his shadow to fall across the potter's face, so that to the potter the sheriff looked like little more than a head eclipsing the sun. "It's a fine morning for a ride," said Geoffrey.

"Such a ride is a gentleman's sport," said the potter. "A lowly craftsman has little time for such a thing."

"And yet you sit well."

"I have an easy understanding of animals, and they have always understood me. Let me return your graciousness, and the graciousness of your wife, with this gift." The potter reached into his tunic and brought forth a brilliant ring.

The circle of gold was warm from its closeness to the potter's body, and the ring was heavy. Geoffrey was well accustomed to guessing the worth of objects, as he was accustomed to judging the station of a stranger. He hefted the golden circlet in his palm and tried to guess what else this stranger had inside his tunic. "My wife has a special fondness for objects of price. She will be grateful, and I thank you."

Geoffrey slipped the ring to a house steward. "I was careful to choose a horse that would give you little trouble."

"You are admired everywhere for your thoughtfulness."

"It's early for flattery, isn't it? Or is it a constant habit with you?"

"A man of your position does not have to be reminded of his worth," said the potter, squinting and then giving up trying to see his host. The potter leaned to pat the neck of the gray horse, running a finger along a black scar shaped like the mark a wet cup leaves on a table.

"Even a wooden sword can do harm," said Geoffrey. "We use that horse in practice. He has been hurt just enough to make him wise."

They rode silently through the streets of the city, and as they left the sight of the castle, Geoffrey turned to look back, hoping to see the watching faces he expected from the slits or from the turrets.

But they had already gone too far.

A half hour was not a precise amount of time. It was a wedge of time, a handful of morning, like saying "a glass of wine" or "a piece of bread." Geoffrey relied on his sense that armed men riding to battle would urge their horses forwards and overtake two casual riders shortly after their entrance into the forest. Geoffrey was satisfied with their easy pace, past chickens and white geese, whose orange webbed feet tracked water from puddles across the paving stones.

A blue-gray surface, the earth rose and fell. Puddles gleamed. Small figures, like clothed fleas, worked in the distance. The sky seemed scraped by a knife, uneven and rough. The horizon was bright, the color of skin. The sun dissolved the clouds as heat dissolves fat. The shadows of the two mounted men spilled ahead of them as they rode, rippling over the ruts and the puddles. A puddle scummed suddenly, like milk, with a sudden breath of warm wind.

A wagon was sunk into mud, and a peasant pushed from behind to help the ox, which rolled a brown eye at the two men as they passed. The peasant stood respectfully, eyes to the ground, and the sheriff wished him good morning.

Beekeepers worked near a field of barley stubble. Their heads were protected by wicker baskets. The flat faces of the wicker made them appear not human as they carried the straw hives. Bees sprinkled the air round them, vanishing and reappearing as the insects danced in and out of shadow.

A bee soared, in the heavy, uncertain flight bees perform, before Geoffrey's eyes, and dodged the potter's head. The fleck of amber continued into the trees, until they could not see it.

"The bee teaches us an important lesson, of course," said Geoffrey, breaking their silence.

"That particular bee or bees in general?"

"Individuals are never important. Only the group

they belong to, the kind of thing, not the specific creature itself."

The potter laughed. "Is that right?"

Geoffrey was mystified. "Of course it is."

"What sort of lesson does the bee teach?"

"Mutual obligation," said Geoffrey, but he had no interest in bee lessons. He was struggling to understand the background of his companion. "We all know why there are so many different creatures." This was the idlest of conversation, standard talk to demonstrate one's literacy, and yet the potter said nothing, proving, thought Geoffrey, that he had no background at all. "It's unusual for a potter to draw a bow as well as you do."

"Yes, it is unusual."

"Like most people, I have a great mistrust of the unusual."

"Mistrust?"

"A great mistrust. Very nearly a fear of it. We all feel this way. The only reason you could peddle your pots, cheap or not, was that it was a tournament day. On an ordinary day a stranger like yourself would have been turned away, and with a curse."

The forest closed round them as they reached the High Way. Birds like chips of steel scattered and hid, and puddles reflected the dark, shaggy silhouettes of trees. A single butterfly, a toss of yellow, struggled at the lip of a puddle of brown water, and the forest made a sound like a long intake of breath.

Great avenues of night clawed holes in sunlight, and ferns stroked darkness as profound as the inside of a lung. Geoffrey watched this side, and then that, each rotted trunk, each glistening mushroom seeming to shift closer as he passed.

"Why do you keep turning to look back?" asked the potter. "I can't hear anyone following us."

"I thought I heard someone."

"There is no one."

"How can you be sure?"

"I am never mistaken about such things."

"Is this the way you came with your cart?"

"Why do you ask?"

"I am curious."

"You know this can't be the way. I came from the north, passing the miller as I came."

"Ah, yes. I had forgotten."

"I had been told that you never forget."

"It seems that you have heard a great deal about me."

"You are well known."

"Where are you going?" Geoffrey pulled his horse aside.

The potter gestured. "This is the way."

Ferns nodded in a gust of wind. Branches scraped each other, and the spears of sunlight dimmed and vanished. Geoffrey's horse followed the one ahead of it through a tangle of fallen trees and naked branches.

There were so many creatures because God wanted there to be many ways man could learn about His power and many ways a man could study the ways to his own resurrection. But why, Geoffrey wondered, were there such cold, dark caverns of wilderness? Why were there tangled branches the color of a serpent's cast-off skin, and leaf mulch blackened with age so thick upon the ground a horse sank into it and had to struggle ahead as through a windfall of dead flesh?

The horses left great hoofprints in the mulch, however, and this meant that the trail would be easy to follow. Geoffrey snapped a branch, trying to be quiet, so that there could be no question which way they had passed. The crack of the branch was a slap in the silence, and Geoffrey's horse shied.

Geoffrey shivered. Surely the men who were following had reached the place where the two horses had left the High Way. He reined in his horse, which tossed its head, more than happy to stop. Geoffrey listened. Wind inhaled through the branches, and a bird the color of mud scurried up the side of a tree.

The forest thickened the ordinary silence, and the thud and crackle of hoof resounded among the scaly trunks. The potter slid to the ground and led his horse into a clearing.

"Where are we?" asked Geoffrey.

"We are here."

A great gray oak sent thick roots across the leaf-red ground. The huge tree had shaped a space in the sky, and the steel-bright sunlight surrounded the tree like a deformed halo.

"The Trysting Oak," said Geoffrey.

"That's right. I knew you didn't forget easily. You understood more than you wanted to admit. Get off your horse. It will be no use to you."

Silence. The thunder of horse breath. The kiss of stiff golden leaf to the ground.

Saint Catherine had been tied to a spiked wheel, which shattered when they tried to tear her body apart, a spike here, a spoke there, all scattered everywhere by divine grace. God chooses to make things known, but He uses events, even the suffering of mortals, to enunciate His truths. Geoffrey was transfixed with the understanding that something was being made known through him, but he did not know what.

The potter pulled a horn, the horn of a beef, gray and luminous, from his tunic. He licked his lips and blew. The note strangled at first and then was clear and hard, and when the note was finished, the sound of slowly drifting leaves was loud, and acorns punched the ground as they fell.

The note echoed among the trees, at once repeated and changed, muffled and furred, like a boulder whose subsequent outlines are disguised with moss, or a coin whose mates are blurred and worn.

And then another far, clear note, perfect as an eyelash.

"Get off your horse, my lord sheriff," repeated the potter gently. "It will be no use to you now."

The sheriff did not move. Not because he intended to flee, but because as long as he did nothing, he would make no mistake. He cleared his throat and swung himself to the ground, ready not to speak so much as to have his throat cut.

The two men looked at each other.

"Who are you?" asked the sheriff.

"Surely you must know who I am."

"I find myself knowing very little."

"I am the same man I was last night and this morning."

"And what do men call you?"

"You know full well what they call me. I am Robin Hood."

21

The forest seemed to take a step closer to where Geoffrey stood, holding the bridle of his horse. The great oak creaked, and leaves fluttered to the ground like parchment torn to pieces and scattered.

An acorn fell to Geoffrey's feet and spun, a lifeless knuckle, food for magpies, and Geoffrey's throat was tight. He thought for an instant of escaping through the forest on the horse, but he remembered the death of his father, stabbed by a broken branch, and stood still in the rising wind.

He would rather die where he was. He gripped the hilt of his sword, whose pommel was imprinted with a lion. He wanted strength to flow into his body from the long shaft of steel, from the hilt, shaped like a cross, and from the emblem of the lion, the most fearless of all creatures, put on earth to remind man of his own frailty.

"I am not surprised," said Geoffrey at last.

"You knew who I was."

"I guessed. I wasn't certain."

"We can be certain of very little."

"I could have held you in the castle, but I wanted all of you, all your men, everything that is yours."

Robin Hood laughed. "I have nothing."

"You have me."

"You are not the sort of man I expected."

Geoffrey was not interested in talk. In his last moments as a breathing man he wanted silence, so he could beg Heaven's forgiveness for all his sins, his grimy, loathsome lusts and fears. Habit, however, the lifelong practice of conversation as a game, made him ask, "And what did you expect?"

"A much different man." Robin Hood walked to one side, appraising the sheriff. "You are not what I expected at all."

"I disappoint you?"

"I am difficult to disappoint."

"How fortunate for you." Geoffrey hated this trading of conversational taps, like pokes with wooden swords, playful and idle, like two pages waiting for their masters to arrive. When his throat was cut, he would experience blinding agony. And yet the years of idle talk carried him forwards. "Most people live lives disappointed in, if nothing else, themselves."

"Is that how people live in their silks and splendid slippers, disappointed in themselves?"

The man was gloating, savoring his victory. Geoffrey stared straight ahead. He would give the man no pleasure. And yet, the man was unarmed. Geoffrey glanced at him. The man's hands were on his hips as he appraised the sheriff, smiling, enjoying his prize.

Could he stand to run a man through, even now?

Geoffrey took a deep breath, into the deep bottom of his lungs. No, he could not use his sword on this man, but this man did not know that. Geoffrey drew his sword, and the gray light made the blade a hard shaft of the winter to come.

"Come now, my lord sheriff. You are not meant for fighting."

As if this man could see into his soul!

"Besides, it would be unwise."

A figure was in the clearing suddenly, without a sound: a man shaggy with ragged clothing and twigs that clung to his stockings and sleeves. The man was panting, but his eyes were as bright as knife cuts, and he held a sword.

The newcomer was huge. He stepped slowly across the complicated roots of the oak and took his place beside Robin Hood. The sword he held was evil with tarnish and hacked and broken along its length so that it resembled a half-thawed icicle more than a span of steel. But the sword was steady in a great fist. The man's knuckles were black with humus and wood grime, and the man's beard tangled with pine needles and earth.

Geoffrey looked up into the swordsman's eyes. So, he thought, this is my death.

Strangely he was calm. It was a weird calm, in which each thorny twig snared in the sleeves of the giant was clear, each whisper of each falling leaf precise and individual. He eyed this huge adversary, who looked like a man shaped out of the forest floor itself, just as God had formed Adam out of clay, and said quietly, "Let me die with my sword in my hand. It will appear more honorable."

"Die? My dear lord sheriff, we will not kill you!" said Robin Hood.

A feeling like sorrow swept Geoffrey.

"You are our guest!" said Robin Hood. "We will hurt you in no way."

The giant did not smile, and the leaves behind Geoffrey whispered, branches moved aside, and bushes shrugged, to show figures everywhere, six, seven men, each holding a bow with an arrow ready-nocked.

"Ransom," said Geoffrey.

"You are," said Robin Hood, "a guest."

"You have disgraced me."

"Of course. But we mean you no harm."

"No harm! You disgrace me in the eyes of men, trap me, hold me—you'd be merciful to kill me here and now!"

Robin put forth his hand and moved Geoffrey's sword aside as if it were a hanging branch from a tree. "I will take your sword," he said, closing his hand over Geoffrey's. "Because if you do one foolish thing, there will be seven arrows in your throat."

His hand was empty. Geoffrey flexed his gloved fingers. Where was Henry? Where were the men armed with lances? They are taking too long, Geoffrey thought, and soon these forest-colored men will slink back into the woods with their prize.

"I offer my compliments to you," said Geoffrey. "And to your men. I had heard that you were cunning, but I had no idea."

"You flatter me, good sheriff."

"By ransoming me, you will destroy my reputation among common folk, and you will earn yourself a fat sack of gold."

"We would not dream of ransoming a guest," said Robin Hood, and he gestured to the shadowy bowmen. Two or three dropped back into the forest, and the sheriff was nudged from behind with a fist, a gentle prod, the sort of encouragement a peasant would offer an ox. "And as to the common folk, don't worry about your reputation among the good field folk of this shire. They already despise you."

"I am sorry to hear this. But I will be even sorrier when Sir Baldwin hears of this and tells the king." Geoffrey stopped himself. Why enhance their pleasure?

But to stop them from hurrying into the woods, Geoffrey added, "Since I am forced into your company, I might as well tell you what leeches you all are, draining the blood from the High Way, asking mock tolls, as if the road were yours!"

"You flatter us, my lord sheriff. And don't bother looking round like that. No one is coming."

"How can you be sure?"

"Your good man Henry and I drank together last night."

Geoffrey's knees weakened.

"He took somewhat more than I did, and I believe he is still asleep somewhere in the castle."

"I am not surprised," Geoffrey said, trying to convince himself. "I was testing him."

But Robin Hood was gone, into the trees like the shadow of a falcon, and Geoffrey was left alone with only the giant and a young man with no teeth as companions. The young man with no teeth nudged Geoffrey as he had before, with his fist, only this time the fist touched Geoffrey's ribs through his cloak. "Hurry, now," said the young man through sloppy lips. "We have much sport in store." The words were mushy: "Shport en shtore." The young man was unshaven, and lean and brown, as if all the fat had been rendered out of him over a fire.

The giant gripped Geoffrey's arm.

"And one thing more, and it please Your Lordship," said the loose lips. The stink of ancient sweat and months of fires and deer fat and pine sap rose round Geoffrey, and he was blind, hooded like a raptor on its way to a hunt.

22

"Of course, it's a hardship climbing over logs you can't see," said the loose mouth. A hand closed round Geoffrey's, and he was helped to his feet. "We'll try to keep you from stumbling again."

The young man was difficult to understand, like a drunkard, but he talked all the more because of that, as if more words were necessary to nail down meaning. "Most of us had to learn to be invisible the hard way, which is by being seen and chased. No one knows how to live as well as a man who has nearly been killed, says Robin."

A branch stabbed Geoffrey's side and snapped.

"Only a short way now, but look out—we're coming to a stream. Be careful of your feet. There are rocks here to step on if you—"

Geoffrey was soaked. He interrupted his own prayer

to the Queen of Grace to curse the lips, eyes, and reproductive parts of the young man.

"We aren't doing it on purpose, Lord Sheriff. If you wore one of these more often, you'd be better at this."

"I should have practiced," snarled Geoffrey.

"Yes, it would have been happier for you if you had, because Robin says that practice is the key to the future."

"Is that right?" asked Geoffrey with elaborate courtesy. "And what other wise things does he offer his disciples?"

"Oh, we'd not be disciples, in so many words, my lord sheriff. Only fellow dead men in a second life."

Geoffrey's feet clattered over flat, loose rocks, and somewhere high overhead a squirrel scolded. The open air of the stream was swallowed as they half dragged Geoffrey over logs so rotten the stink of wetness rose with each sinking step. Moss fur was at his fingertips, and mud built up under his nails, making his fingers feel large and numb.

It was like being lost in a gigantic, wet tapestry, wandering up and over the individual fibers of the cloth. There was no sound but the rasp of three men breathing and the brush of feet though ferns. Geoffrey felt himself slipping, and he put a hand out to a tree wet with slime, and then another hard and scaly as a snake. Flakes of tree hide came off under his fingers, and he cringed, staggering forwards.

"Not too much farther now, my lord sheriff, and then you'll enjoy the most welcome feast you've ever had, and there can be no question about that."

"No question at all," said Geoffrey through clenched teeth.

"We all have something in common now, my lord sheriff, and that's the truth on it. We all thought we were going to be dead, but we're alive, and that's the great wonder, by the Mother of God."

The strange, clumsy words had sounded very nearly pious, and Geoffrey groped past a tree before he asked, "When did you think you would die?"

"Many times, and it please you, so many times, but most especially when your own men caught me for a chicken thief, although I was innocent as a cow's knee, and it please you."

Claims of innocence always made Geoffrey suspicious. "Perhaps you had decorated your fingers with hen feathers to amuse your friends."

"No, my lord sheriff, I was as bare of even a speck of hen dirt as anyone since Adam, and your men held me to the ground, as Heaven is my witness, and pulled my teeth with a smith's tong."

"Ah."

"And I saw myself dead and gutted, my lord, in pain though I was, except they left me to swallow blood and be rescued by Robin and taken to the greenwood, where I still am, by the grace of our Lord."

"I see," said Geoffrey, stumbling.

"And you thought you'd be dead, under the Trysting Oak, didn't you, my lord? Oh, you put on a good show, but I saw that shiver down your back when I stepped out behind you. I saw those neck muscles thinking on their future, which they thought would be primarily shortened by a bit of forester's steel."

Mollified by the slim compliment that he had "put on a good show," Geoffrey said, "I did wonder about my future."

"Wonder! There was naught but a certainty what you were thinking, and we all saw it. But don't think twice. We've all been afraid before and lived to tell the tale."

Before he could muster a response, there was a familiar voice, and for an instant Geoffrey was glad to hear it. "You've arrived at last," said Robin Hood.

"And a most perfect companion he has been," said the toothless one.

The hood was tugged free, and Geoffrey blinked.

The giant was still at his side, a full head taller than Geoffrey, who had always been vain of his good height. No doubt, thought Geoffrey, this man's tongue has been pulled out. A great fire crackled round a log like the legless carcass of a horse, a huge, misshapen chunk of wood. Glistening faces studied him, pausing over simple tasks, mending a stocking, hammering a metal bowl with a stone, rubbing a bowstring with wax. The boughs of pines suggested a roof, and the arcing, blackened ribs of a boar suggested a previous meal.

"We are pleased to welcome you," said Robin, removing his cap in a graceful bow. He was in different clothes now, but they were, if anything, more ragged than his potter's garb. He wore a stained leather jerkin and a tattered skirt that once had been green.

Rude tents stretched over bedding. Straw scattered among trees had been squashed into mud. To Geoffrey's horror he saw that some of the dirt-black faces were those of women. A grease-shiny hand searched a head for lice, and another used a knife to squash a tick that had fled a fold in a cloak.

"Your companions were never introduced to you, a lapse for which I apologize," said Robin Hood. "The young man with the willing tongue is Will Scathlock. The large man at your elbow is Little John. Over there is Much, son of a miller, and I would introduce all the rest, but I fear you might misuse the information. Many of these people have families somewhere, some of whom pay us a visit sometimes. We look like animals, but we are not."

It was the point in a conversation at which the guest said something like "Oh, no, you look nothing like animals," in the time-honored exchange between self-deprecating host and courteous guest. Geoffrey simply stared.

"Please sit and let us entertain you. We want nothing more than to serve your pleasure." Eyes everywhere glittered with interest, and every face seemed to know everything about him, as if he had been there many times. "You see, we have a place prepared for you."

Geoffrey sat on a deer hide, and a hand with nails black as claws handed him a goblet. The silver was dusky, and the mouth of the goblet was bent oblong, but the red wine was good, stolen, no doubt, as pavage from a merchant.

"We have been waiting for you for a long time," said Robin Hood. "Because in a way you belong here."

"As happy as I am to be here," said Geoffrey—and

in truth, he was happy to be anywhere—"I don't know why you feel I belong with you."

"Oh, you don't, actually." Robin's eyes twinkled as he sat and poured himself wine from a chipped clay pitcher. "We belong with you, in your chamber, between your sheets. But since you would not have us, we must have you."

"What did you do to Henry?"

"Nothing. He reeled from your chamber, already forgetting what you had told him to do, and I finished him off with a few pitchers of new ale."

"It was that simple?"

"As easy as the telling of it."

"I trusted him."

"Don't think about it. We would have had you one way or another."

23

It was probably still day, but it made no difference here. The fire was bright, and a buck was brought, hanging from a pole, its antlers dragging twin lines in the earth. The beautiful eyes looked into Geoffrey's. A single spot of ripe blood over the animal's heart showed where an arrow had hissed and taken the world away from the deer.

The deer is me, Geoffrey thought, and when the gutting knife glinted in the firelight, Geoffrey could not watch. Never before had the carcass of an animal shaken him like this. "You serve good wine," said the sheriff.

"Only the best," said Robin.

"My men would have devastated this little band."

"They have done their best already. Shorn ears, chopped hands, gouged eyes." Indeed, even as he spoke, the pink bud of a clipped ear protruded from lank hair in a nearby tent, a sleeve fell away to expose a stump, and a sightless eye pursed itself tighter.

"Tell me," said Geoffrey. "Where did you get the pots?"

"Certainly you don't think I stole them."

"Why not?"

"I bought them from a traveling potter. I paid him well, and he was pleased to be rid of his wares."

Yet another deer sizzled over coals, and Geoffrey made a sour smile. "You help yourselves to the king's livestock."

"We would be very hungry otherwise," said Robin Hood.

When a slab of venison steamed before Geoffrey, and his glass had been filled, Robin Hood said, "What entertainment would you like? A battle with quarterstaffs perhaps? We are the best in the shire at staff-battles. It is, after all, the weapon of the peasant, and most of us are common."

"I think not, but thank you."

"An archery display!" said Robin Hood.

"No, I have seen enough of that."

"Then a story."

"Very well. A story."

"Little John," called Robin Hood, "tell us a story."

The huge shape of a man detached itself from a tree, and the great tree-colored figure stood before them.

"We want a story, Little John."

The giant looked deep into Geoffrey's eyes, as if reading something there.

"And since we avoided a fight today, let it be a story

of battle," said Robin Hood. "Let there be swords in it, and blood."

Little John's eyes glittered in a face like a mossy bole. He closed his eyes and stood unmoving for a moment. Then his eyes opened again, and he slowly raised his arms. The forest itself seemed to grow silent, and only the fire whispered.

"Kanut was a warrior," said Little John, his voice deep and clear. "He was a mighty swordsman. No one could defeat him in battle. His sword flashed like the noon sun, and blood pattered on the ground like piss.

"One day Kanut's lord commanded him to travel to a distant land where they needed the service of his sword." Somewhere a hand stroked a lute, a discordant, quiet sound. Little John stared hard into Geoffrey's eyes, then raised his arms again. "A distant land, where he was to rescue the countryside from a monster.

"Kanut set sail across the sea in a storm, the water black and tossing, and gulls wheeling across the sky. When he arrived, he knelt and thanked Our Lady for his safe passage. The shore was a waste of sand and seaweed. The sky was the color of iron, and the farms were a tangle of weeds. Kanut walked the road with his sword in his hand, because the wind stank of death. There was silence, except for one sound: the sound of a woman weeping.

" 'What can trouble thee?' asked Kanut. 'Fair maiden, answer me what grieves you.'

" 'A monster has destroyed this land,' she said. 'It has gutted the men, burned the hayricks, and left only myself to weep, so that the loss might be felt by one survivor, one person who remembered the world as it used to be, when men laughed and women sang.'

" 'Where is this monster?' asked Kanut, shaking his sword. 'I have come to kill him, and I will not leave without his head.'

" 'He lives in the cave beyond the Blue Marsh,' answered the maiden.

"And so Kanut found the Blue Marsh and crossed it in a scull, working his way across water that clung to his pole like paste. Birds cried through the air with a sound like infants bawling, and the sun was a stab in the sky.

"Kanut stood before the cave, sword in hand, and called, 'Come forth, beast. I have come to slay you.' A flock of transparent sheep trotted forth from the cave, a herd of intestines and brains. But Kanut knew devil's work and stood his ground. 'Come forth, beast,' he called, and a train of maidens came forth, beautiful and fair, singing in the voices of very old men, 'Kanut, mighty among men, who fears no creature, leave us to our peace.' But Kanut knew devil's work and stood his ground. 'Come forth, monster, that I might slay you and be finished.'

"The wind stopped, and the herd of sheep and the beautiful maidens vanished. The clouds glowed like heated iron, and the sun was as pink as a scar. And then a child came forth, a little child. Kanut waited for the child to transform itself into a dragon, or a griffin, or a manticore, but the child took Kanut's hand and said softly, 'I am the beast. Kill me.'

"And Kanut prayed, 'Mary, Queen of Heaven, I cannot kill a child!'

"But the child said, 'Kill me or I will waste more, and savage the world with my devouring.'

"And Kanut prayed, 'Jesu, Prince of Paradise, I cannot kill a child!'

"But the child said again, 'Kill me, for no evil done upon this land does not flow from these arms, no rapine does not come by these hands, no sorrow except by these fingers, this child's form.'

"And Kanut slew the child before another word was spoken, with a single blow, his blade slicing the child as easily as a stick slicing wind.

"The Blue Marsh cleared, crystal bright, and the scull was transformed into a barge of silk and damask, and the perfume of flowers was in the wind.

"Ruddy-faced farmers embraced Kanut, thanking him for their deliverance. And their wives embraced him, thanking him for their lives, and the elders of the village embraced him, thanking him for returning them to the world.

"But Kanut threw his sword into the sea, and dropped his shield upon the sand, and let his chain mail slump to the jetsam of the shore, because he had killed a child and had no more taste for battle."

Little John turned slowly and picked up a knife and cut himself a chunk of venison. He sat and ate. The spice of the meat was in the air, and a drizzle began to fall, a small rain that made the band of men and women huddle in their cloaks.

"A good story!" said Robin. "A magnificent tale! What do you think, Sheriff?"

"A good story."

"And what lesson does it tell?"

"I have no idea."

"You were telling me the lessons of the bee—"

"That was something I learned in childhood. I have never heard this story before, so I can't guess what it might mean."

"And you'll never hear it again. He made it up, on the spot."

"He invented it?"

"Yes. Here and now."

Geoffrey shook his head. "What a strange thing to do."

Robin smiled, chewing and wiping his lips with the back of his hand. "You never invent anything, do you, Sheriff?"

"I invent traps that fail."

"But you never create anything new, something that was not there before you."

"I don't understand."

"You do not make things up."

"I am not a craftsman," said Geoffrey disdainfully. "I was never intended to work with my hands."

"You are too good for that," said Robin.

"Besides, I didn't really like the story." He paused to see if anyone acted offended, but everyone chewed, seeming to ignore him. "It seemed pointless."

"How was it pointless?" asked Robin.

"It seemed so to me. Ask the storyteller what it was supposed to mean."

"Oh, Little John almost never talks, unless to tell a story."

"He never speaks a truth, then," said the sheriff peevishly.

Robin laughed so long Geoffrey stopped eating and pushed away his wooden plate. Robin wiped a tear and said, "Never tells a truth!"

"I amuse you. This is not surprising. This must be how you derive pleasure from your captives."

"Forgive me, my good lord sheriff, but you are an amazing creature. A talking mute! A seeing blind man! A dead man with moving arms and legs."

"I am glad I please you."

"I expected a burly man, a man who was cruel but also fiery. A man filled with fury and hatred. I expected a man of muscle and little wit."

Geoffrey tasted his wine. "And?"

"And I get a dry man."

He said "dry man" as he might say "dried peach."

Geoffrey gathered himself. "A pity that I disappoint you."

"I am delighted! I see so few like you! You are a piece of furniture! You are a door knocker, a stirrup! You have lived so close to duty that your soul has shaped itself to it, like a glove worn so long that even when the hand is gone, it still has the full shape of a hand."

"A guest should delight his host."

"My good lord sheriff, I do you wrong. You have a muscular soul. You have fears and hopes. But"—Robin leaped to his feet—"you should laugh! The world, the very world, is pointless, just as Little John's tale seems meaningless. The story of all of it makes no sense, tells no lesson, makes no one wiser; it is a smear of honey

141

pricked with flies, and a man who frowns all the time takes no more pleasure than the bee working from flower to flower, every day until he turns into an empty thimble."

"My host is a philosopher."

"Music!"

The lute jangled, and somewhere in the dark a bag-pipe squeaked. The squeak swelled into a drone, and the pipe bleated as Geoffrey winced. Robin danced well, Geoffrey conceded to himself. The lute broke a string, but the bagpipe continued. Robin danced beside the fire, and Little John joined him, prancing like a frenzied bear.

"Dance, my lord sheriff!" said Robin. "Life is an inch!"

Geoffrey smiled grimly and sat where he was.

24

The sheriff woke. He could smell morning, a gentle stirring in the air, but it was still dark.

Geoffrey sat up, and the pine needles beside him crackled. He looked up, into the deep-set eyes of Little John. Little John placed the end of his quarterstaff on Geoffrey's chest, and Geoffrey lay flat again.

A night bird cried, a sharp, passionless scream, without fear or fury. His guard was gone, but Geoffrey sensed the men round the camp and cursed the darkness. How he hated night! And how easy these men seemed in the dark, at home in it, wearing it like disguise. He lay still, an organ in a gigantic, sleeping creature.

The darkness was rotten, a gray patch of mold spreading high above them. The charred logs lifted a single white thread of smoke. A figure stooped over a single red tooth and dropped a handful of shavings.

"You're awake," said Robin Hood.

Geoffrey searched himself like a man who has just fallen. He groaned to his feet. "What are you going to do with me?"

"Are you still afraid?"

"Not anymore," he answered truthfully. "Something about a new day gives me courage."

Robin laughed.

Geoffrey took the crust of bread he was handed, a chunk the color and shape of a chunk of peat. He chewed, and sipped wine from the icy metal goblet. "My men will run you to the ground."

"Such confidence, so early in the morning."

"The wisest thing for you to do," said Geoffrey, "would be to run me through, this moment, with your sword."

"I knew you would have an eye for this," said Robin, holding the blade into the drizzle. The bright steel was unblemished, the sword of a knight. "I was given it by a traveler once."

"Most yeomen don't know how to use a sword."

The pines dissolved in mist. Water pattered from the black boughs, and the world was gone. There was only this knot of blanket under a veil of smoke. The air was ripe with wood decay and a human odor, sweat and wet wool. There was a smell of horse manure from beyond the camp, and the crack of an axe.

Robin slipped the sword back into its scabbard. "I don't know if we will ever see you again."

"How many times have I seen a hound kill a rabbit

by shaking it once, like a rag? And how many times have I seen a pack of them tear a rabbit to bits?"

"Threats, my lord sheriff?"

"I wish you luck."

"I will keep your fine horses, and thank you for them. In exchange I give you back your sword and this gift—"

Will Scathlock grinned toothlessly, leading a fine white palfrey.

She was beautiful. Slender and powerful-delicate, in that breathtaking way of the finest mares. She accepted Geoffrey's touch, giving over to him peacefully, her pink nostrils playing across the pine needles, puffing some of them aside to expose the dark ground.

Suddenly he was in darkness. The hood rasped over his ears, and the voices round him were distant, words in a dream. Whether he left the band or the band left him, he could not tell. His sword was buckled into place, and he was helped onto the palfrey. His hands were tied behind him with coarse rope.

Branches crackled, and the horse felt its way through the forest. "Who's with me?"

"Only myself, and it pleases Your Lordship, leading you through the greenwood, since a man can scarcely ride when he can't see."

"You don't have to live here anymore," said the sheriff. "Why don't you come back to the city? Robin Hood and his men are doomed."

"Every man alive is doomed, good Lord Sheriff," said Will Scathlock. "Every man breathing is only waiting for the thread to break, and that's certain. Besides, forgive me, you'll never find us."

"Never?"

"Can you find fleas, Lord Sheriff, except they find you first?"

"Leave them, Will. Your head will end up on a pike if you don't."

"My head is little more than a turnip, at best, Lord Sheriff, and that's the truth."

"My men were unjust to you. I understand this. But that's no reason to abandon the world."

"And who's abandoned the world? The greenwood is as real as any tapestry, forgive me, and a deer is as tasty as a ram. Don't worry about me, my lord sheriff, and don't worry for a moment about Robin Hood. You might as well spend your worry on a cat."

"I wasn't worried," said the sheriff. "I don't like to see unnecessary death."

Until the end he knew an arrow could stop his breath. Until the end he half expected the sound of a sword singing through his ribs. But after what seemed a day of riding blind his bonds were cut.

"Take it off now. You're free," said the toothless mouth. "And a good day to you."

Geoffrey blinked, wadding the round dark cloth in his fist. He was alone. The High Way opened ahead of him to stubbled fields. A crow glinted like black glass, and a rut was filled with a long, slender puddle the color of steel, a lance of water that reflected the gray sky.

25

All day Hugh labored with the wooden sword, making Ivo sweat, lunge, parry until at last the old swordsman had to resort to a a hip throw to knock Hugh down to the straw-littered floor.

Later Hugh helped Ivo with an inventory of caltrops, large balls with spikes of iron. The spikes were rusty, never used, and Hugh helped Ivo chip away at the red glaze, long into candlelight. The spiked instruments were used in battle, scattered in streets to discourage war-horses. Hugh was glad to help Ivo, but the young man could not help thinking of the forest, the nightmare forest, and the real one, the one that had swallowed the sheriff.

Geoffrey did not return by the time the beeswax candles were stubs. Lady Eleanor paced the halls, glancing from window to window. Hugh stared at the dying fire in the great chamber and at last crept off to his pallet, to lie sleepless.

Every rustle of nesting pigeons, every sneeze of stabled steed, was surely the sheriff returning. Hugh prayed to Our Lady, asking that her mercy guide the sheriff and keep him from all harm.

By dawn the castle stirred, servants-in-waiting whispering, distant roosters cheering the sun.

But the familiar voice, the familiar step never came.

THE CREAM-COLORED WALLS of cottages were bright across the gray ground. The brown thatch of roofs matched the just-harvested fields. The wicker hives trickled bees into the cool noon, and the well cast no shadow, its handle chuckling as Geoffrey cranked. He drank deep from the water scoop.

A peasant dog wagged its tail, and Geoffrey massaged its head through its tangled hair and worked a spear of wild rye out of its ear. The peasant himself shuffled to the well, hat in hand. "Day to yer'dship," said the peasant.

The peasant stared after Geoffrey as Geoffrey turned to look back, surveying the dark wall the forest made, pressing up against the peaceful fields. The cut the High Way made in the dark cloth was a tiny opening, barely a slit, and all round the fields, and all round the city in the distance, bright with its windows and chimneys, the forest was waiting.

The thief was still hanging from the gibbet, but the

clothes hung loose now, and a carrion crow folded itself over the skull like a great black book of prayers.

The drizzle began again, the gray wool lowering over the city. Drops of water small as dust fell over the palfrey's mane. Geoffrey's sleeves looked floured for a moment and then darkened as the water soaked in. The walls of the city were grimy with damp, like the sides of a sweating horse. The market was strangely empty, except for an orange cat that stared and fled.

Geoffrey tickled his spurs into the palfrey, and she eagerly leaped into a gallop. A duck fled in a burst of white feathers.

The gatesman called, "He's here!"

Only the swans ignored him, grousing among the greasy weeds of the moat. Ivo, the furbisher, ran across the courtyard in his leather apron, and Hugh clutched Geoffrey's leg. "I prayed for you, my lord," said Hugh with a fervor that brought tears to Geoffrey's eyes.

"I'm glad to see you, Hugh. Where's my good deputy?"

"Henry's gone forth with a crowd," said Ivo.

Geoffrey allowed himself a thin smile. "Has he? But not you two, the best of the castle."

There was something canny in Ivo's expression. "I recognized a fool's errand even as I fastened on my sword, my lord."

"Ivo and Hugh are the only men I can count on not to be fools," said Geoffrey.

He gave the reins to a horse steward, an old man who was nearly weeping. "Take good care of her," said Geoffrey.

LADY ELEANOR HELD OUT her hand and did not let Geoffrey's go. "I thought the worst. Indeed I couldn't sleep."

Geoffrey took each step slowly. "I have a gift for you," he said.

"I can't imagine—"

"It's a white palfrey, very dainty but strong in her way."

"You seem so strange."

"Do I?"

"So—so strange."

"I have spent a very pleasant night. Whyever should I seem strange?"

"For God's sake, you haven't disgraced me—"

"Ah. I can see now why you were worried."

"Forgive me, Geoffrey. I know you have more discretion. I just—I was very worried."

"You can stop worrying," said Geoffrey. "I am quite safe." He paused at the doorway to his chamber. "Hugh, please send Sir Roger to me at once."

"He's gone, too."

"What!"

"He said that Henry was too much an idiot to lead men in battle, and he put on his breastplate and helmet and rode out ahead of them all."

"But the saints help us—he's not well." He meant: he was too old.

"He looked," said Hugh, "magnificent. I saw him as he must have looked outside Jerusalem, standing in his stirrups to count his men."

"I hear good news from all sides." Geoffrey smiled. "I come home in triumph to hear that everything is well organized and that not a trace of panic has touched the castle."

"Please don't look so terrible," said Lady Eleanor.

"Terrible! My dear, I am the picture of calm."

"Too calm. Hugh, leave us."

"Hugh, stay. I will need new clothes. My study gown. I don't think I will be going forth today."

She took his hand. "Please tell me what's happened," she whispered.

It was a long time before Geoffrey would allow himself to answer. "What has happened is that Henry, the man of my right hand, is a virtual traitor."

"No!" The word *traitor* had an ugly sound. Traitors were disemboweled and made to look upon their own intestines before losing their limbs and eventually their lives.

"Not, of course, quite literally. Although I am by proxy the king, he escaped actual traitorhood in all but intent."

Lady Eleanor was pale. Geoffrey sat, and Hugh unfastened the spurs. "But," said Geoffrey, "as you can see, I am quite calm."

Geoffrey stayed in his chambers, wearing the soft green gown he liked to wear when he studied. He had a large book of tax numbers before him, but he was actually studying a second, much smaller book, which he had sent Hugh into the tower library to find. In this manuscript the Archangel Michael poised in the air over a city. His white wings were spread against the blue sky, and a beast of gold had just been stabbed by the

151

sword the angel brandished. Blood ran in an alternating pattern in twin lines of drops, but the blood did not reach the city; it seemed to evaporate in the air.

Horses clattered into the courtyard. Geoffrey stood and paced and then forced himself to sit. He could not sit! He was up again. "Who is it?" he called to Hugh.

Hugh left to find out. By now messengers must have reached the search party. Certainly an army of mounted men would not be hard to track. Geoffrey marched round the room. Certainly his men had not lost themselves in the forest. That was quite impossible. But they should be here by now. Not just a few horses clattering into the castle, but dozens of them.

He stared at a wedge of cheese and a green apple, both untasted. He picked up the paring knife once again. Even with this little knife, he thought. Even a knife so small could gouge out the tongue of Henry, Henry the faithful, Henry the loyal tanner's son. Or perhaps Nottingham the executioner would devise some supreme punishment for a man who slept away his duty like a gorged sow.

Hugh waited at the door and would not come in.

"What is it?" Geoffrey said.

"It's Sir Roger."

"Send him here at once. I want to see him."

"He can't come." Hugh's voice was peculiar.

"What's the matter?"

"Sir Roger is dying!"

26

Geoffrey hurried with Hugh into the barracks.

"It's his heart," said the physician.

"Sir Roger deserves more comfortable quarters than these," said Geoffrey.

"He asked to be carried here," said the physician.

"Then build a fire," said the sheriff evenly.

"We—we don't want him too warm," said the physician. "He is too hot and dry as it is."

Hugh was struck by the trace of nervousness in the doctor's manner. The physician was rarely startled or caught without some supple, easy answer.

Sir Roger put out a hand that was pale and mottled. "God struck me down," said the old knight. The stricken man's blouse was spattered with dried peat.

The sheriff knelt and stroked the old warrior's brow.

"God could feel nothing but love for a warrior like you, good Sir Roger."

"Did you catch the jack-in-the-woods, that robber?" asked Sir Roger.

Geoffrey stood and met Hugh's eyes. "Not yet," he said.

A SOUL IN PURGATORY could be released when thirty trentals had been sung. Those who sung these masses were almost always paid for their labor, and it was marvelous that Heaven and Purgatory and even Hell were anchored to this world, as weft and warp are anchored to the frames of the loom. The living souls were the ones that seemed most trapped of all, although perhaps this was a sinful thought.

The candle flames were like golden eyes, watching him. He closed his eyes and let them watch. He was empty of all deception. He was empty of everything, a man ready to begin his life again, to take orders or be hanged.

Even as a boy he had felt responsible for things that went wrong. There had been the usual boyhood games, of course, including Geoffrey's least favorite, Dun's in the Mire, in which boys grappled a log, trying to pull it from the outer chamber into the sunny courtyard. It was a game that always ended in scrapes and, among the younger boys, tears. Geoffrey had learned not to cry, but he had never been convinced that all that wrestling was anything but a waste of effort. He had enjoyed then what he enjoyed now: being left to look at manuscripts in his father's library.

He left the chapel. The drizzle had stained the paving stones, and his footsteps left dry kisses across the courtyard. The castle smelled cold and stony, like a quarry. A fire crackled in his bedchamber, and he gathered the gown round himself, studying the tax numbers idly, the vellum whispering in his fingers.

Horses thundered into the courtyard.

"Hugh?"

As always, the quick response, like a speaking shadow. "My lord?"

"Have Henry come to me at once."

Hugh's feet made almost no sound on the floor, only the smallest hint of someone passing, the sort of sound a thought makes when the mind turns away from it.

Geoffrey sliced the apple not because he was hungry but because he wanted to cut something. The seeds were dark, the color of old blood, like the dried blood of Christ Geoffrey had seen once, red-black silt in a silver vial. The scent of apple was in the air.

Henry knelt.

Geoffrey set down the paring knife very carefully. It made a metallic chime on the brass plate, a tiny peck of music. Geoffrey stood and walked round Henry as he knelt, unmoving. The man smelled of wet leather and pine needles, a combination like a field during rain. Geoffrey circled Henry once, then returned to his seat.

Already the apple was losing its whiteness. Brown touched the edges of the white mouth in the fruit, and one of the seeds had slipped from its place, leaving an empty socket, a seed sheath.

"Not long ago I wanted to have your tongue fed to dogs."

Henry did not move, his head bowed.

"I could think of no punishment harsh enough."

Geoffrey picked up the apple and put it down. He waited for his deputy to speak, but the man remained silent, crouched like a man unable to move, doubled like a fist.

"Stand up so I can see you."

Henry rose slowly but would not meet Geoffrey's eyes.

"I know what happened," said Geoffrey. "Robin Hood told me."

The very name was magic. Henry cringed and put a hand out to the wall. He shook his head and tried to speak. His voice made a dry croak, like the grunt of a swan.

"I want to hear your voice."

The man shook his head and groped along the wall.

"Speak to me!" Geoffrey hurled the apple, and the fruit exploded on the opposite wall. The sheriff paced. "I command you to use language."

Henry swallowed. He made a noise like a cow lowing in a distant pasture.

"What?"

"Sorry."

"Sorry!"

"Terribly sorry." The man shrank to the floor again.

"Get up. I don't like to see you crouching like a frog."

Henry stood, but held himself like a man with a cramp.

"I will tell you what happened, and all you need to do is nod if I am correct. You had a bellyful of ale before you came for your instructions, and a bellyful afterwards, with our good friend the potter. When you woke late the next morning, swollen like a boil, you remembered nothing of my instructions. Am I right?"

Henry nodded, a kind of spasm. "Hugh woke me."

"I can't hear you when you mumble like a dog."

Again a spasm. "Hugh woke me."

"Thank God for Hugh. At least I have someone about me I can depend on. And you should be thankful for him, too. If not for Hugh, you might still be asleep!"

Henry shivered.

"It's hard for me to recall when I have been more furious. You are, as a deputy, very nearly worthless. A man of straw would be more useful. At least from such a sack I would expect nothing. I wonder if you deserve the chance to redeem yourself."

"Anything I could do," mumbled Henry.

"Many sheriffs would have you hanged. Without discussion, without even a syllable, and without a breath of remorse. Your conduct was very nearly traitorous to the king's will. You know this all too well. You put up a show of duty, but you think about your own skin more than anything else, don't you, good Henry? There are those good men who would condemn me for talking to you at all. The king himself would probably flay you." Geoffrey paced. "Well, you must have had mixed feelings when the messenger found you. He's alive! Wonderful news! Now I can hang!"

Henry slumped to the floor again.

"Oh, by the love of Jesus, stand up or I'll unman you with this apple knife, as surely as I'm a Christian!"

Henry said something anguished.

"What?"

"A terrible disgrace."

"Ah, yes. Disgrace. Well, my dear deputy, I have been disgraced, too. And it's not entirely your fault. No doubt Robin Hood knew exactly what he was doing when he tilted the pitcher of new ale." Geoffrey sighed. "I guessed who the potter was. I should have had a better plan."

"I'll do everything in my power to bring you the head of Robin Hood."

"No," said Geoffrey thoughtfully. "I don't want his head, and I want any of them you catch brought to me alive. I think some special punishment would do them justice, something for Nottingham to discover, something that will make them regret the day of their birth."

"We will make them suffer!" said Henry, climbing to his feet.

"They expect us," said Geoffrey. "Even now, they are in the forest, listening. Waiting. They may even have spies in this city, watching to see what we do. But we will have no secrets. We will have nothing to hide. You, Henry, will eat, rest." He did not say "drink." "And then you will take your best men, not an army. Your best. And you will run them to the ground."

27

eoffrey put down his slice of simnel. "Why do we have to listen to that ugly noise?"

"It's a psalter," said Lady Eleanor.

Lady Eleanor's maid-in-waiting plucked at strings with a quill. She hesitated.

"I know exactly what it is."

"I'm sorry. I wanted music. Please," she said to the young woman. "We have changed our mind."

Since his return Lady Eleanor had been more gentle, and Geoffrey wondered if, in fact, she had been worried about him. She had dressed with great care for their first evening meal together since his reappearance, and the pearls round her neck were lustrous and made gentle clucking noises as they rubbed together, pleased with their own beauty.

Geoffrey did not like music, except for the music

that preceded a disorderly person to prison. A minstrel usually led a miscreant through the streets. This called attention to the punishment and made it all the more shameful.

"No, you can stay," said Geoffrey. "I am," he said to his wife, "perhaps a little tired."

"Of course you are. What a dreadful thing to spend a night out there."

They were both silent, sensing the forest everywhere round them.

"How is Sir Roger?" she asked.

"He is asleep. He is happy in that cold place, surrounded by bucklers and axes and, by now, cursing men. I gave Henry orders. The men will have to curse quietly."

Geoffrey became aware of a strange figure at the edge of the firelight. The figure wore a metal bowl over its head and held a long, crooked staff. The figure was evidently on guard, watching over the meal. Geoffrey asked the server, "Who is that?"

The server met Eleanor's eye. "That," said Lady Eleanor, "is the Fool."

"Why is he wearing that pot on his head?"

"It's not a pot."

"Why, it is a pot! An insult in my own dining hall!"

"It's not a pot; it's a metal bowl. Please do sit down. I'll send him away."

"No, don't send him away."

"Geoffrey, you are behaving in a very strange manner."

"Strange! Then at last I am in a mood to enjoy the

Fool's company. Come forward, good Fool, and let me see you."

The Fool marched to Geoffrey's side.

"Yes, just like a man-at-arms. A lance, or is it supposed to be a *langue de boeuf*? That would be a weapon for you, my dear Fool, a spear with a tongue at the end for the easy removal of your opponent's liver. And a helmet, missing, of course, the noseguard that keeps a point from reaching your brain by way of your face."

The Fool knelt, so quickly and so quietly it seemed a genuine apology for upsetting the sheriff.

"Go!" said Lady Eleanor to the Fool. "Geoffrey, please have some more wine."

"No, stay, Fool. You find helmets and lances something amusing, or perhaps it's me you find ridiculous, held like a stolen ewe in the greenwood, with a band of greasy thieves, waiting for my throat to be cut."

"Geoffrey, please."

"I'm ready to laugh! Ha-ha! See how I'm laughing!"

"Geoffrey," his wife said, her voice a hard whisper. "I will not allow this!"

"Everyone finds the Fool amusing except me. I intend to be amused. I intend to be cheated out of my awareness of the world until I laugh, and why not? In my own household, a man in my castle among men."

"You are amusing me," said his wife shortly. "I laugh to see the lord high sheriff in such a good humor, such high spleen, such a dry and heavy-handed fool himself."

Geoffrey gripped a silver goblet until it closed in on itself. He said softly, "I have long wanted to see if the

Fool has a tongue. This is the night my wondering will cease!"

Lady Eleanor's eyes were fierce. "Geoffrey!" she said. "The Fool is your servant!"

Geoffrey strode across the hall and stormed down one corridor, and then another, through darkness and candlelight, until he stood at last at the top of the East Tower, the wind streaming through his hair. Where is there a capable servant for me! he thought. Where is there someone who can do my bidding, even if it's simply to talk!

Chain mail jingled, and Geoffrey was aware that he was not alone on the tower. "Good evening, my lord," said the spearman.

"It's a cold night," said Geoffrey.

"So it is, my lord," said the guard, using the local *swa* for *so*. "And more to come."

"Yes," said Geoffrey, as if he knew.

"But tomorrow we'll catch Robin Hood that lives in greenwood and drag him hither."

The burls and thorns of the man's speech calmed Geoffrey. "I am glad to hear it."

"What is he but a man, and a mortal man at that? He'll not last, though the people say he'll hide until Judgment Day. Trust a man who's seen many a thief at the end of a lance, some breathing, some not. A smart rabbit, my lord, is nothing but a rabbit."

Geoffrey felt his way down the steps of the tower. He bumped someone, and a body fell with a gasp.

"Hugh!"

"I was looking for you."

"Why? What's wrong?"

"Nothing, my lord."

They groped their way down a corridor. "Don't you want to hear what happened?"

"My lord?"

"Don't you want to hear what happened in the forest, with Robin Hood? Everyone wants to know, but everyone is afraid to ask."

"What happened?"

Geoffrey laughed. "Nothing."

"Nothing?"

"I ate king's venison and drank good wine. And then they let me go." But as he said it, it sounded worse than torture, worse than injury. It made a mockery of hospitality and made mock of all hosts and all guests, everywhere.

Hugh's cheeks burned with gratification: the sheriff was confiding in him! But other emotions seethed within Hugh as well: embarrassment at the treatment the lord sheriff had received. Anger. And determination.

It was a heady thought, one Hugh would not have put into words. He was, after all, only a greaver's son.

But some sunny morning Hugh would make Robin pay for his crime against the sheriff.

28

I fear the worst," said Geoffrey as Hugh fastened his rowel spurs. "Sir Roger is too peaceful. His vital virtue has fled."

Hugh was shocked at his own speech: "I want to ride with you."

"This is not sport, Hugh." And then the sheriff himself was surprised. "How can you learn if you stay in the castle today?" But your safety is a weight I carry, Geoffrey wanted to say. Your life is mine to protect. "Perhaps the two of us together can make Henry feel his duty."

The blacksmith worked at his anvil, using the hammer with a long, tapering point and a blunt, squared face. This face flattened the red slug of iron. Red sparks kissed the leather apron. The smell of hot iron was the smell of power flowering into frailty. The definite and concrete were becoming fluid.

"We will ride with you," said Geoffrey. "At least part of the way."

Henry tugged at his belt and looked down.

"I mean no criticism. I thought I could help."

"We will be proud to have your assistance, my lord."

Henry had organized a dozen men, sturdy, helmeted, and doomed to fail. Geoffrey surveyed them with satisfaction. He must try to catch the highwayman. It was his duty. And perhaps, although he did not expect it, they might blunder into Robin Hood. It was not impossible.

Boys played in the marketplace, using sticks with strings attached to set tops spinning. The dark shapes like turnips wended between the stalls until they reached the feet of a haggler, rolled, and fell still. This seemed to be the point of the game, and the people in the market seemed not to mind it, as if boyhood were a nuisance that would pass on its own, like flies, and could be endured until time did its work.

The day was bright, and the wind cold. Oxen fed in the common land, the wetland reserved for grazing because it was too muddy for anything else. The beasts grazed, great four-legged outcrops of earth carved to resemble animals.

A few tufts of clouds dirtied the sky, and the horizon was a crisp line of earth and sky, like vellum newly torn, still shaggy where fiber had not worn. The High Way was wrinkled with cart tracks. Grass made the sound of men walking through the fields, although it was only the wind. The wild grain nodded and stood erect again.

"Here," said Geoffrey at last. "This is where we left the High Way."

"Horses will be a burden in there," said one of the men, whose green tunic showed him to be one of the king's foresters.

"A horseman is by his nature more powerful than a footman," said Henry.

"Not in a brake of brushwood," said the forester.

Geoffrey made a gesture, and there was silence. "The men you are looking for are like no men you have ever seen. They are not knights, and yet they could unhorse one easily. They are not foresters, and yet they use the greenwood like a pantry. They are to us what men in a dream are to real men. They inhabit the woods like thoughts and flee the approach of light, like nightmares you try to remember but cannot. These men are insubstantial. Any one of us could batter any of them.

"You will not have the chance unless you hunt them as you hunt fish with your naked hands. Be still, and listen. Do not grasp what is not already giving itself over into your hand. Strength is no assistance. Woo Robin Hood, like a maiden. He wants to show himself, so he can taunt you. Rush him, and he will entertain the lot of you, as he entertained me. Seek him like knowledge, gently. If you hear him, don't turn to look at him, or he won't be there. Look away, and say, 'Greetings to you and your band from the Sheriff of Nottingham.'"

They entered the greenwood. The horses broke branches, struggling, as though the path taken by Robin

166

Hood and Geoffrey had closed, healed like a wound. The ripe, wet stink of forest was everywhere, and when Geoffrey put his hand to the side of a tree, a tree-colored moth broke into the air, fluttering at his eyes and lips.

They searched for hours before they discovered the Trysting Oak. It looked unimportant now, smaller. Brown leaves fluttered to the ground, and the massive roots wrestled the earth beneath a blanket of leaf mulch. The leaves dissolved as soon as they reached the ground into a kind of leaf silt, formless and dead.

Geoffrey's instructions on how to find Robin Hood could have been the instructions on how to obtain God's grace. It could not be obtained. It was only given. Uncalled, it came like an owl in the night, tawny and moon-gray, seeing everything by the light from a single star.

They led their horses over gigantic moss-rotten logs. At times the horses broke through the crust of humus, like horses struggling through black snow. Even the forester stumbled, and searched the ground for tracks, finding only mushrooms, shiny and domed, like the heads of babies buried upright in the ground.

"They filled in the tracks," said the forester at last.

"Even so, there will be traces," said Henry. Henry was at home here, searching and sweating. He was most comfortable when he was sweating. "They are men, not birds."

The forest was dim and silent. They were aphids shut into the pages of a vast dark book. At last Henry lifted a finger and knelt.

A branch had been lopped off, leaving a stump ending

in midair. "Axe," said Henry simply. "Not long ago. Two weeks, maybe less."

Geoffrey fought a smile. "So we are only two weeks behind them."

Henry sulked.

"Still, it is strong evidence that they do, after all, exist," said Geoffrey.

"We'll find your camp, and then the next one, and the one after that until very gradually the noose tightens," said Henry.

A branch poked into Geoffrey's tunic, a long, skeletal finger. "I can't help thinking they are watching us even now," he said.

"Let them watch," snorted Henry. "They'll see what a band of stout men looks like."

The horses splashed a stream. Geoffrey touched the water and nearly slipped. "Yes!" he whispered. "Yes, this is the right way."

The pine needles were russet, and the pine trunks as stark as trees that had been charred. Only high overhead were there any leaves. The ground fell into gentle culverts, and Geoffrey pulled his horse ahead of the men, studying the ground, searching, trying to sense the path.

He hurried ahead, past one tree so much like another he had to turn back to see his men following, with Henry ahead of them, stout Henry, reading the ground as he could never read a book.

"I've been here before," Geoffrey breathed. "But it was so different. It was like years ago, like something I saw when I was a child. Where was the fire?" He turned to Hugh. "They had a fire. Perhaps here, among these big trees. And a deer was hung up somewhere. And there were tents."

Henry and his men held back. Finally Henry suggested, "Maybe another place, farther on."

"Perhaps. I can't tell."

Henry knelt beside the forester. "I don't see how twenty people could have camped here. Not even a year ago."

Geoffrey searched forwards, and he was there. The deep shadow, the scoop of land—all changed. There was no trace of a fire, not even a speck of charcoal. Geoffrey spun, doubting and then reaffirming. "This is the place," he said, "But it looks so different."

Henry knelt and sniffed the ground. "Are you sure?"

The forester dug into the earth with his fingers and brought forth a piece of charcoal like a coal-black arrowhead.

"I'll leave you here," said Geoffrey. Henry had to regain his pride, and searching without the sheriff would be medicine to his self-assurance. And Geoffrey could do no more. Every tree was a shaft of darkness.

29

Geoffrey huddled, shivering in the privy in a tower over the moat. He wiped himself with a handful of hay and let the hay fall down the dank shaft on the tower. What a pity you can't build a fire in the privy, he thought, although you could send for a brazier of coals. A starling had worked its way into the roof of the castle and chattered, imitating the laugh of the carrion crow, the low of a cow, and the sound of a distant horn, a steer horn blown by a huntsman announcing that he was killing one deer for his own use only and should not be arrested. It also sounded strangely like that other, sonorous note that had brought the figures into the shadow of the Trysting Oak.

Hugh helped Geoffrey out of his nightgown. Geoffrey stepped into his linen underpants and let the gown of soft wool fall over him, to the floor. He wore a tunic of coarser wool over that and a belt of ox leather. He pulled on a cap of black wool and tied it under his chin against the chill.

Hugh brought a pan of steaming water, and Geoffrey let his hands steep in it, a brass dish nearly overflowing with summer, or with the heat of those distant places where men had no heads but had eyes and mouths in their torsos, and were thereby so much more difficult to kill.

Geoffrey had one case before him today: a freedman, who made a living catching bream in the river, had blackened the eye of the bailiff when that officer had arrived to collect taxes. Geoffrey sat as judge for such cases and prepared himself carefully, always. He wanted to know who the accused was, who his father was, and how the accused got along with his wife. A bitter wife made a bitter man.

THE FREEDMAN WAS LEAN, the coarse cloth of his trade hanging on him like flags. Bream hunting was apparently not a way to get fat. The man's eyes were downcast, and the manacle on his wrists jingled as he fell to his knees.

"Stand before the law," said the clerk.

"Your father was a huntsman. Charles was his name . . ." Geoffrey began.

The mention of a man's father made him either stand taller or shrink. This man shrank. "Indeed, my lord, he was a master of snare."

"Yes, I remember seeing your father's snares at work.

A rabbit, running in midair, going nowhere because a thong gripped his hind leg. And they call you Tom."

"Yes, Lord Sheriff."

"Your father was killed by poachers."

The man did not move. "Stabbed through the skull, my lord," he said quietly.

"These men were caught, and drawn, and quartered."

"I remember it well, my lord," said the man without raising his voice, a thin figure whose past and future collided to crush him.

Geoffrey, too, remembered, the smell of blood as the writhing men were shown their own entrails, the smell of blood and the stink of offal in the early-morning air.

"This household," the sheriff continued, "is a steady contributor to your income. Last Friday we spent seven pence on salt flounders, fifteen pence on mullet and bar, and the Monday before that we spent twelve pence on bream. So that when our bailiff goes forth to collect his tax, we expect him, if respect for law is not sufficient, to be accepted courteously out of respect for us. Every seller in the market pays us a tithe; you are not the only taxpayer."

The freedman was pale, a thin carving in bone.

"The customary punishment is the cropping of the ears. Such punishment makes you a spokesman for the rest of your life on the power of the law. A punishment does two things: it cures the criminal, and it advertises the cure to the world, as a warning."

The manacled man said nothing.

"But we understand that you and the bailiff were old

adversaries. We understand that your defiance was not of the law but of this bailiff's person. This is still an ugly matter, but not as ugly as rebellion against the king's tax. Therefore, your tax will be tripled and paid at once, or your body held in chains until your friends and family can pay it for you.''

Geoffrey waved the man away.

"A perfect justice, as always," said the clerk, showing his teeth.

"There is perfection only in Heaven.''

"There is one other matter, although it does not really concern you.''

Geoffrey waited.

"The miller was nearly killed yesterday. Knocked flat, and still as a dead man for two hours, although now he is awake and cursing, as always.''

Geoffrey covered a smile. "Whatever happened?''

"A bear he had bought for bear-baiting, an old, pie-bald beast waiting to die like an honest animal, was tied to a stake while the dogs were brought." The clerk beamed. "And the rope broke.''

"The rope broke!''

"Snapped! As much to the surprise of the bear as anyone, from what I hear. The bear looked this way and that way, and then, seeing that he was no longer tethered, ran straight into the miller.''

"A wonder he wasn't killed!''

"A miracle.''

"And what happened to the bear?''

"The miller's son shot sheaves of arrows into it and chased it as far as the forest. I doubt that bear will bother anyone but—'' The clerk had been about to say, Robin Hood.

"YOU SAID YOU WANTED to see me, and then you were nothing but busy.'' Lady Eleanor drifted into the room, her blue silk gown making the sound of wind in a pine.

"The fact is,'' said Geoffrey, "I have been reluctant to talk with you.''

She lifted her hands to adjust her wimple, a frame for her eyes and mouth, and her pale cheeks were brightened with just a touch of Parisian powder. "Whyever should you be reluctant to talk with me?''

"The falconer must go.''

"He is nothing to me—''

"Then I will get you another.''

Her eyes were downcast. She turned away. "I am having a pendant made,'' she said. "It will depict the death of Saint Thomas à Becket. I think it's important to remember that the saints were human and that they suffered.''

"The world is a brutal place,'' said Geoffrey.

"And the abbess?'' said Eleanor lightly.

"What does that mean?''

"A garden,'' said Eleanor, "shut off from the rude world is not safe.''

"What garden?''

"We try to concentrate peace into portions of the world because we cannot have it everywhere. And the world intrudes on this peace, rushing it, like a flood.''

"Whatever are you talking about?''

"Pigs! I am talking about pigs! They invade the abbey garden."

She toyed with the blue silk. "When you were gone, all that night. When I sent to find out if you had come in, and word was always 'Not yet,' I realized something. Something about the way I felt. You are my husband, and in that estate of being your wife I do not have to love you."

"No. You do not."

She said, after a pause, "But I do."

HUGH HELPED IVO WRAP the sword pommels with kid leather, holding the blades firm while the swordsman worked.

"What of smaller swords?" Hugh asked. It was a question he had been saving, unsure when to ask.

"No need to worry yourself about the fisher blade or the poacher's steel," said Ivo absentmindedly. "A Christian broadsword is fit for you."

"But don't some warriors dagger their enemies?" asked Hugh, slipping the ox-hide gloves from his hands.

"What do you want with a dagger?" asked Ivo, looking up, his fingers stained with tannin, his eyes bloodshot from working by cow tallow candles.

"I should know how to use a shortsword. Like that dagger above your bench," said Hugh, indicating a black blade gleaming on the wall.

Hugh had been afraid to ask, sure the swordsman would disapprove of such a secretive, ignoble weapon.

"I want you to learn to fight," said Ivo, "not to murder."

But what if there was someone in particular who should die? thought Hugh. An outlaw whose continued existence was vile.

30

The falconer attached the jess the bird already wore to a long, black leash, talking all the while in a voice like the speech of a dove, a low voice that the falcon turned to hear better. "Night Hand, we call her, and Night Hand she is to rabbit. No one sees her come." He interrupted his human speech to speak like a dove again, and the falcon shook itself, lifting the feathers round its head into a mane.

The falcon saw Geoffrey again, its eyes so intense Geoffrey stepped back. This bird could love nothing. For it, there could be only killing and not-killing. The killer-bird looked away from Geoffrey, cocked an eye, and looked back at Geoffrey again, its talons finding a new place on the glove.

And the falconer smiled, the sly smile of a man who

has great skill. "She obeys only me, and she will do whatever I tell her."

"A proud creature," said Geoffrey, feigning boredom.

"The best," said the falconer. "She will attack anything at my command. Anything at all."

"I am amazed at her, I must admit."

"She will attack even a man."

Geoffrey forced himself to smile. "Such a bird could blind a man easily."

"Easily, my lord."

The bird tightened its feathers again, reducing its size by a third, its head turning to view Geoffrey like a knife with eyes. The falconer spoke to it in his bird language, and Geoffrey could not breathe. The creature was like a crossbow, loaded and cocked, held in the falconer's hands, and Geoffrey felt for his sword, knowing that if the bird leaped, there would be nothing he could do.

"We will sell the falcons and offer your services with them. I will have no trouble. The birds are magnificent, and you are highly skilled."

The man continued to purr into the ear of the falcon, and the bird cocked its head, listening as to long instructions. The gentle voice spoke of only one thing to the bird: killing and the taste of killing and the feel of flesh in the beak. "You will regret your loss," said the falconer.

"Undoubtedly."

"Night Hand!" whispered the falconer, and the bird stood erect and still. "Night Hand!"

"But my wife tires of these birds."

"She is always so merry out under the sky."

Geoffrey stepped to the bird and spoke to it himself. "Night Hand will fly as beautifully for another master."

The bird ruffled its feathers again. The bird had accepted Geoffrey's voice, the sound of its name in Geoffrey's mouth unlocking something in it, as a key unlocks a chest. The bird lifted the talon that was not encumbered with a jess and scratched its head.

"Night Hand trusts you," said the falconer, with a tone very much like disappointment.

THE PHYSICIAN PICKED UP HIS BASKET. "Does the rue still affect you?"

"I have not thought of any woman for quite some time."

"When again you feel passionate thoughts, begin taking more of the rue. The body becomes accustomed to our treatments, just as we become accustomed to cold in winter."

"Just as our bodies become accustomed to death," offered Geoffrey.

The doctor smiled, but it was a tired smile, and Geoffrey realized that the doctor was not a young man, far from it. The man's eyes were red, and his gray hair fell over his forehead.

"You're doing your best to save Sir Roger," said Geoffrey.

"You sound surprised."

"Oh, no, dear doctor. I simply forget that—well, forgive me, but I forget that you are human. You seem so perfect in manner." This was only a half-truth, but

Geoffrey was ashamed to realize that he did not like the surgeon much.

"Sometimes," the doctor said, putting down his basket, "I wonder if we know anything at all. About the body. About the world."

"Does the miller recover?" asked the sheriff.

"Yes, that crafty simpleton, if such a creature is possible. He should be dead. That beast, bear, bull, or devil knocked him flat, trod on his chest, and left the good miller bruised everywhere."

"Everywhere?"

"Essentially. The man cannot move. He drinks ale and curses. He is a pitiful sight."

"He will recover?"

"Of course, although I have little sympathy with millers. They take a sixteenth of all the grain milled and cheat in the weighing, I am almost certain. I suspect the miller is as wealthy as I am." The doctor blushed at the mention of his own wealth and stammered, "But he will recover to cheat again, I assure you."

"Now I can sleep without my dreadful fear that the miller might not recover," said Geoffrey.

The doctor chuckled again, quietly. Geoffrey was surprised to find himself enjoying this man's company. If only, in the back of his mind, he were not eaten by anxiety regarding Henry and the forest. What was happening out there, in the greenwood?

The two gazed out into the courtyard. As they looked on, Hugh marched alongside Ivo, gesturing, acting out a stabbing gesture, while Ivo shook his head.

"Your squire, Lord Sheriff—"

Something about the man's tone troubled Geoffrey. "He doesn't look ill?"

Sometimes a fever struck while a person was unaware, still going about his duties. "No, dear sheriff, not ill. But he looks too intent on his duty, too drawn into his labors."

"He has much to learn—"

"Be careful that he does not become swallowed by his office and turn into another colorless grown man, like your clerk. Like myself, if I may say so."

Or, thought Geoffrey, like me.

31

That evening a messenger arrived from the forest. The man was black with mud. A splotch of it shined above his eyebrows like a dark eye looking out of his head, contradicting everything he said.

Henry was driving the men hard. They slept as little as possible, cursing the night for being so long. And they had good news: they had found a recent camp. So recent a deer hung just gutted, and the ashes still glowed. They had blundered on it by accident and had plainly surprised the outlaws. "They were only minutes ahead of us," said the messenger with a grin.

Geoffrey ordered the best meats for the messenger and praised Henry. But why was this news painful? For a reason he could not guess, Geoffrey did not like the idea of Robin being surprised.

"This was deep in the forest?" Geoffrey asked at last.

"Very," answered the messenger, chewing. "Halfway to Barnsdale, it seems."

So Robin was not lingering near Nottingham. Geoffrey repeated his praise of Henry, but when he stood at the top of the East Tower and looked across the city to the darkness, he was not glad. There was something wrong.

As he stood there, smelling cooking fires and the dirty water of the moat, he looked up at the starry sky, and a meteor curled across the sky, slowly, like an eyelash burning. Geoffrey looked down, then leaned heavily against the battlement.

MANY YEARS AGO a peasant woman had stabbed her husband through the lung with a kitchen knife. The man, through the power of the saints, had run into the road accusing his wife, before he collapsed and died, screaming bloody gouts. The woman had been condemned to the gibbet. But the previous sheriff, a corpulent man who had no pity for any living thing, had suffered a mercy cramp and decreed that she could live, provided that she would be walled up in a tiny house near the graveyard for the rest of her days.

Such a building was mortared, and the woman was led to it accompanied by priests, and the place was consecrated. She was shut up in it, and the only opening was a small slit, three fingers wide, for light, air, and the food of awed villagers. She did nothing but pray, constantly. Her crime was virtually forgotten. The sheriff was long since dead of a tangled gut, and the priests had faded into age and fallen. The holy woman survived, praying, and, when asked, offering a prophesy.

Geoffrey did not like to think about her. It was terrible to be locked into a standing grave—worse than locked; a gang of men with sledgehammers would have to free her, and they might well crush her in the process. It was better to think of her as dead, as a spirit trapped on earth, like a moth in a cupped hand. Besides, only very common people sought her help, and while there was no shame in doing so, it was nothing to be proud of, either.

But Geoffrey had seen a meteor, and a meteor meant only one thing: death. It was the surest omen.

It was cold by the cemetery, and the stars were too bright, as if eager to overhear. A wind started and stopped, and Geoffrey's breath joined the breath of Hugh in a sloppy wreath round them both.

The black slit in the stone wall was directly ahead of them. Such a small building, scarcely bigger than a privy. Geoffrey did not want to look at it. "She's probably asleep," said Geoffrey, tucking his gloved hands under his arms for warmth.

"She never sleeps," whispered Hugh.

"How do you know?"

"We talk about her all the time, everyone I know."

Geoffrey nodded.

There was a cesspit pungency in the air as the slit exhaled. Geoffrey crept close to the slit and put his hand on the moss-hairy wall. "Stand away, so you can warn me if anyone is coming," said Geoffrey, who actually did not want to be overheard.

Geoffrey was alone then, leaning against the wall, a

wedge of waxy cheese in his gloved hand. Wind took in a long breath and held it. It was colder, and the stars were clear and hard, ice on black water.

A common person, used to imploring, would know how to begin. Geoffrey had no idea. The smell of the cheese mingled with the stink of human dirt, but Geoffrey was familiar with unpleasant smells.

A saint you simply prayed to. With this holy woman there was a potential for give and take, and the thought disturbed Geoffrey so much he wanted to leave at once. It had been a reckless thing to come here.

Endless whispered words, too soft to hear, as gold hammered air-thin is too pliant for anything but the finest altar. The prayers were urgent, too, like those of a woman who had only minutes to live, not at all like those of someone who had been praying for twenty years.

"Good woman," whispered Geoffrey, "I have brought you some food."

The quiet prayers grew faster. They were like the shuddering imprecations of someone tortured nearly to death. The presence of such holiness pressed Geoffrey against the wall.

In an instant the cheese was gone. Vanished, as a spirit would vanish into an opening in the fabric of space. And the prayers stopped. There was silence, black and perfect as a moat at night. Then they began again, even more quiet, and if he had not heard them before, it would have been impossible to hear them now, as soft as green leaves blown across grass.

"Good woman, I need your help."

The unseen lips continued their constant whisper, but the sound grew brighter as the lips approached the dark cut in the stone. She was there, listening as she prayed, on the other side of the stone. Geoffrey shivered. "I need your help," he repeated.

Again silence, like a third person between them.

"I have seen a meteor, and I need to know: am I about to die?"

A glistening white twig appeared on the stone sill of the slit. Another joined it, and another, fingers in the starlight. "God's palate," she whispered, like an unusual curse a knight might make, but so fervent Geoffrey knew it was not a curse. "God's precious wounds."

And the woman wept.

"Please, good woman," said Geoffrey. "Please, don't cry."

"God's precious tongue," the woman keened, and Geoffrey began to cry, too. He knew why the woman wept, seeing before her like a presence in the room the terrible agony of Christ. Geoffrey pressed himself hard against the wall, so the stones hurt. He wanted to ask her to stop crying, but it was futile, because he knew she had good reason to weep, naming the tender parts of Christ's body, and weeping at the terrible agony He felt. The two of them were locked in the horror of it.

And the shame, that mortals were so unworthy. It did not matter to Geoffrey whether he lived or died. His life swam like the sheen on the skin of a bubble.

HUGH WAS WAITING, just beyond earshot. The two of them hurried away from the churchyard. High on the wall a guard shifted his spear, turned, walking his rounds.

"God gave me a sign this night," said the sheriff. "A sign that I am in mortal danger."

"Did the anchoress—" Hugh could not bring himself to ask. Geoffrey had never felt so close to Hugh, nor had he ever felt how impossible it was to express his tangle of fear and faith.

"My lord," said Hugh, "I will protect your reputation and your life with my own."

The intensity of the young man's speech touched Geoffrey, but it concerned him, too. And somewhere in his mind there was a touch of affectionate amusement as well. What can you do, dear Hugh, he wanted to say, that all my men and all my prayers cannot bring to pass?

Geoffrey surprised himself by saying, "I know you will."

32

The Fool stood in a shaft of morning light. The alert eyes followed Geoffrey as he paced. In the Fool's hands was a kind of sceptre, but a very grotesque sceptre. A stick of wood ended in the neck of a head, like a pike into the neck of a criminal. The head resembled the head of the Fool himself, but smaller. The Fool carried a severed Fool's head—perhaps a charm against beheading, but in Geoffrey's eyes a reminder of what he deserved.

"Because, as I told my wife, I feel that we should have a discussion," the sheriff continued. "I have asked someone to join us, briefly. I want you to get to know this castle, and my responsibilities, better than perhaps you do now."

The calm of morning mass still lingered in the sheriff, but as he paced and talked, he felt the last of it dissipate. The thing in the Fool's hands turned and was watching.

"Because a sheriff is not simply another man, to be admired or mocked. A sheriff is in a position to do terrible things."

The Fool's head on a stick had lifted to the level of the Fool's shoulder. The Fool's face was a mockery of alertness, and the smaller face was a mockery of that, an exaggeration of an exaggeration. It had wide white eyes and red lips.

"Terrible things," said the sheriff. "Please, have some wine." The Fool declined with a gracious gesture, more courteous than speech, and the head on a stick made a flourish in the air. Geoffrey poured himself some wine, purple splashing into the goblet with a sour sound.

Geoffrey frowned over the rim of tiny bubbles and drank. The Fool watched, a mask of patience and interest. "I apologize for the way I behaved towards you. It was inexcusable."

The Fool made a self-deprecating bow.

"I was tired, of course, and mad with—well, not mad. Sick in my heart with rage. Rage that I no longer feel. But as master of this household I should never speak to a servant in that manner."

The small head watched him.

Geoffrey consoled himself that he was wise enough to know how to apologize and wise enough to know when to stop. "And now I think the time has come for you to know me better. I don't say, you notice, for me to know you, because I have never heard your voice."

Geoffrey allowed himself a smile. "You are always silent."

The small head was rapt.

"Silence is a subject I understand better than you think. Silence is everything, speech is nothing, just as the blackness of the sky is profound and rich, poured out like iron over everything. While stars, those tiny specks of light, are almost nothing. When something is almost nothing, it becomes very important.

"A world of silence. Forest and brake, field and river. At best, the grunt of a cow, or the murmur of a fly." He said "fly" directly into the eyes of the small head, and the thing seemed to understand, seemed nearly to smile. Disheartened, Geoffrey plodded on. "So you see how important it is that people talk. Without talk we have only the bare, cold walls. We have only the wind and the sky, and—what is that devilish thing? For the love of Jesus, put it away!"

The head bobbed and trembled, and the Fool consoled it. He rocked it like an infant, while the sheriff looked on, appalled. He put his hands over his head, to make sure it was where it was meant to be, he supposed; he didn't know why he was doing anything.

"Speech," continued the sheriff, pacing again, "and its counterpart, silence, are of special importance to the sheriff. Because if the sheriff wants to know where something is hidden, and who else helped to hide it, he must crack the nut of silence and extract the morsel, the little truth, that only speech can deliver."

The Fool hugged the head across his breast and gazed

upwards at Geoffrey from the place where he had fallen to his knees, in an attitude of reverence.

"And so he learns how to make people talk." Speaking of himself in the third person was a great comfort. "He does not enjoy this, but he has no choice."

Geoffrey gazed into his wine cup and saw a purple, quaking vision of himself.

"Yes, send him in at once," said Geoffrey in answer to the announcement of his second visitor, but he continued to gaze into his wine, at the bubbles at the edge of its surface like blue pearls.

Immediately he knew it had been a mistake. He should have tolerated the Fool, pretended to enjoy the Fool's company, and gone about his business. But it was too late. The other visitor had arrived.

"A pleasure to see you, my lord," said Nottingham.

"It's always a pleasure to see you," said Geoffrey. "I was simply telling my Fool how little we love silence."

It was uncanny the way Nottingham and the Fool resembled each other. The same small bones, the same lean faces, and yet the Fool looked infinitely more graceful. Nottingham bent sideways when he spoke, as if trying to see round Geoffrey, round everything. "Silence is a secret's castle," said Nottingham.

"Amazingly well put, good Nottingham. Tell us the ways to make a man talk."

Nottingham eyed the Fool briefly, then looked back with a thin smile. He made his eyes open wide for a moment before he spoke, telling the sheriff that he understood. "If a man wants to keep silent and remembers who he is each moment, it can be difficult to make him talk. Oh, he will bawl and bleat. But the only way to make him speak is to make him leave himself behind, like an empty sack. When he has been stripped of himself, then he will talk."

"When he is naked of any disguise."

"Then he talks." Nottingham's eyes were quick, burnished by the sights they had seen.

Geoffrey turned and spoke as if to the tapestry of the falling warrior, the wounded figure composed entirely of silk and wool. "Tell us some of the ways you allow people to forget who they are."

"Many ways, as you know well." Nottingham glanced at the Fool, assessing the Fool's silence, estimating the time it would take to melt it away. "I need not mention the rack, and the tong, the fire iron, and my most recent discovery, the lapping goat. These are really for people who merely hesitate before speaking, not for people who have determined that they will not speak."

Nottingham waited for encouragement, but Geoffrey did nothing more than touch the tapestry with a forefinger. The tapestry was so thick he could not feel the wall behind it. The multicolored cloth was like the hide of an animal with muscles of granite.

"For those determined silences, we favor slow burning or slow cutting."

The "we" made Geoffrey clasp both hands together. "And?"

"They both involve time. The slow burning is like death burning, but the fire is built a good distance from the criminal. The flesh ripens, blisters, and begins to char. The man talks. Slow cutting is a method I do not favor. The time involved, and the number of men. You have no idea how annoying it can be. And the mess— needless to say, it is not my favorite form of speech loosing. A rope is stretched across the chamber and made as taut as any straight line you could draw. I take two stout men—two stout and very patient men—and we slide the criminal back and forth across the rope, back and forth across the room, until the man is cut in two." Nottingham made his hands part, like two wings. "Although generally he speaks long before he is actually in two halves. Such men forget who they are. They seem to be giving birth to something. They can never believe that such a thing is going to happen to them." Nottingham's voice became almost thoughtful. "And it doesn't, in a way. By the time they talk, they have become little more than a bloody tangle."

The Fool remained on the floor, looking away from both men.

"No one," Nottingham continued, "has ever been cut in two in that manner, at least in my experience. It simply advances to a point where it doesn't matter, like a hot knife into ice."

"Do you," said Geoffrey in a low, hoarse voice, "sometimes wish you were someone else?"

Nottingham straightened. "I have been trained from boyhood not to indulge in wishful thinking."

"Thank you, Nottingham, for joining us."

He flinched. He had expected, no doubt, a long visit,

even some wine, and then perhaps an opportunity to demonstrate his powers. "It is," said Nottingham, "an indescribable pleasure." His phrase made something tighten in Geoffrey, and he did not move as Nottingham made an ugly bow and faded towards the door. The man did not leave at once, his lean face looking back, expecting, it seemed, a summons to return and to describe yet another example of his skill, the skill he had learned from his father, as a tanner learns to cure hides, and a cobbler how to craft them into boots.

The man was gone, leaving a strange scent in the air. Geoffrey could not place it as he strode to the door to shut it securely, because Nottingham had left it just open, deliberately. The door shut as gently as a book, and Geoffrey recognized the smell: it was goat.

Geoffrey raised his fists before him in a helpless gesture, but the Fool was not looking. He crouched on the floor, his eyes downcast, still holding the head on a stick like an infant.

"I have to have things done—no, allow me to speak the truth plainly. I have to do things that are hateful to me. It is like a vow. Like a vow of silence. If the law will not go into a man, I force it. Sometimes the law is not language and money. Sometimes it is a team of horses that pulls a man into the air like a spider, until he rips apart."

Neither man moved for a while. Geoffrey usually loved his chamber and did his best thinking there. Now the room was too small, and too cold, as a damp wind breathed into the room from the floor, from every uncovered chink.

"I want you to know this about me. I have a weakness: I am not cruel. I think that I wanted you to be afraid. Threatened. Thinking that I could have your flesh broiled until I found out everything about you."

The Fool cast a vague shadow about himself, a smudge of Fool shape round him on the stone. The little Fool cast an even smaller shadow, but strangely distinct. The toy was more real than the man.

"I am sorry, Fool. I could never do these things to you."

The Fool stood, and this time his face was not a caricature. It mocked nothing. But the eyes were bright, as if Nottingham's spirit had entered the Fool as he sat there on the floor. Except that the eyes were not the eyes of Nottingham. Alert, but unguarded. With a spasm Geoffrey realized that the Fool was hiding nothing. Still, Geoffrey could not read the Fool's face. Had he been afraid?

The Fool's homunculus hung straight down, a hammer at rest. The look in the Fool's eyes became clear to Geoffrey. The sheriff glanced away.

It was the look of compassion.

"You aren't like us," said Geoffrey. "You have already escaped and left yourself naked." He put his hand on the Fool's shoulder, but heavily, so that the Fool would see that Geoffrey was not merely gentle. "Be assured, Fool, that I will do you no harm. And be welcome to your silence. Leave now, before I begin to hate you again."

The Fool balanced the head stick on his forehead and spread his arms. The toy head smiled at Geoffrey.

"Very good." He sighed, feeling ridiculous, as if he had to console the wooden head as well as the human one.

33

Ralf, the chief huntsman, checked the knot on a rabbit snare. The rabbit inside the net kicked and flattened its ears. "Easy now," said the huntsman, "easy, at your rest."

The white rabbit was still at the sound of the huntsman's voice. The man could calm as easily as he killed. The burly huntsman was beyond both cruelty and passion, just as a dog is beyond such feeling and will kill or save with the same eagerness. "The rabbits are ready, my lord. My best beaters are ready. And it's a beautiful day for a rabbit hunt, if I may say so."

This was a long speech from Ralf, who usually kept to short sentences and, when he was hunting, shouts like "There now!" and "Hoy!"

A dove pecked seed scattered on the stones of the

courtyard. The laundry wench shielded her eyes to see Geoffrey on his horse, and Geoffrey looked away, quickly.

Lady Eleanor joined them, at last. Geoffrey had promised her that they could go rabbit hunting but did not look forward to it. It was only fair that if she could not go falconing, she could go hunting in some other way. But Hugh was sick with an ague he must have breathed in on the cemetery air two nights before. The doctor had given him a tincture of vervain, but the youth was not well enough to ride.

"You look well this morning, Lady Eleanor," said Geoffrey.

Still no word from Henry. And now, with Hugh taken ill, the sheriff felt himself surrounded by cares. Perhaps the meteor had foretold the loss of Hugh! But the surgeon had been reassuring, promising that the fever would pass in such a vigorous youth. Geoffrey wished he could believe it. Sometimes the sheriff woke at night and heard the laugh of Robin Hood.

Some of the netlike snares held other creatures, animals as lithe as the rabbits were soft, arm's-length beasts with short forelegs no longer than fingers. These shapes whipped and surged in their nets, and bright teeth sparkled in the sunlight. They had been still until now, asleep, surrendering to the boredom of courtyards and horses.

But now they saw the fields, and smelled the rabbits, and they would not be stilled by the huntsman's low voice. The brown, snaking shapes assumed the forms of all the letters of evil magic as they struggled in the hands of the huntsman's beaters. The huntsman looked to Geoffrey, and Geoffrey nodded to his wife, indicating that her pleasure was to be served.

"Yes!" said Lady Eleanor. "Let the rabbits go!"

Rabbits were everywhere, kicking across the grass. Each rabbit stopped, dazed, for a moment, by freedom. The beaters took their places at the edge of the field and drove an errant rabbit back. The rabbits stood upright, working their noses, and then wandered, feeding.

The snake creatures with the brilliant teeth were insane, lashing their nets from the inside. Even the horses quickened at the sight of the frenzy and shied, wide-eyed.

"Look how excited they are," called Eleanor. "Let the rabbits spread out, and let some go into the nettles over there, where they'll be more difficult to catch."

Geoffrey tugged his gloves on more tightly and chewed his lip. He fiddled with the shortsword he wore and scuffed the ground.

"Now!" cried Lady Eleanor.

Nets were shaken open, and the ferrets were in the field. Rabbits streaked and bounded across the grass, but the ferrets were invisible, dark arrows that seemed to speed nearly underground. A rabbit kicked, its white fur suddenly pink. Another screamed, and the beaters struck the nettles, as everywhere in the field rabbits struggled and went nowhere.

Lady Eleanor clapped her hands. "It's wonderful!" she cried.

"We'll be eating rabbit tonight," Geoffrey noted dryly. "They certainly make quick work of it."

A rabbit's scream was so unlike the cry of an animal—an undiluted cry of terror. The beaters worked the nettles with their bush sticks, flat, club-shaped paddles. The men called to each other, pointed, and laughed. The huntsman, who had seen this a thousand times, jumped up and down, pointing and cheering.

Geoffrey smiled wearily at all of it. He loved Eleanor in her pleasure, but he could not share it. "Will you please excuse me from this frolic?" said Geoffrey. "I will walk in the woods for a moment."

"Of course," said Lady Eleanor, not bothering to glance at Geoffrey and declining to note the tone of his voice. Geoffrey, like most men of reason, did not enjoy walks in the woods. Only his contempt for such a hunt could drive him away.

Immediately the other world had him again. The shouts of the beaters were silenced, and the laughter of his wife dimmed and went out like a candle consuming the last spoonful of its wax. Sun filtered through the branches, and he was in emerald air, trapped in it and yet wanting it, believing that in this amazing beauty he, too, could be beautiful.

He slipped into the darkness under a tree and held his breath.

He was not alone.

He loosened his shortsword in its scabbard. He had seen a figure, an indistinct presence. He crouched, to make himself smaller and to listen closer to ground level for the crush of pine needles and the snap of twigs.

Another fly moaned through the air, slowly, because it was late in the year for flies. The sound of its passage was lost in the whisper of wind high above. Geoffrey did not move. He should, he reasoned, call out. He was armed, although not heavily. It was probably a forester or even a poacher. A poacher would be terrified of the sheriff, Geoffrey told himself.

He kept his silence.

A step, there, behind the trees directly before him. The dry syllable of weight taken off pine needles, a single, definite sound. Someone was waiting for him.

The day had fallen away, like a cloth stripped from a bed to expose a naked thing. The morning existed only here, his hand on his sword. He had been brought here, by God or by the other unseen powers of the universe, for this meeting. He knew that.

But he did not know what to do. He wanted to speak, but he did not know what to say. And anyone who would hide, cowering behind trees, was not worth addressing.

He drew his sword. The shaft of steel left the scabbard with a sound that itself would be a warning. The sword reflected the forest dimly, a gray, blurred reflection, a tear in reality itself through which he could see another, duller reality. He strode round the stand of pines and cleared his throat to speak.

A shape uncoiled and threw itself high over Geoffrey, towering, and a roar like the crashing of a great tree froze him. A limb fell down upon Geoffrey, crushing every thought.

34

e could still see. He could not move his arms or legs, but he could look upwards with open eyes and fail to comprehend what was happening. A hellish monster rose high over Geoffrey, a shaggy thing, a chunk torn out of midnight. The thing fell down over him. Small eyes, red-black, like silver tarnish. Twin spouts of hot breath, and the sour stink of an old dog, decay and saliva. The huge thing eclipsed the day, and Geoffrey saw only black fur, and the heat of the thing was everywhere.

The thing grunted, and teeth tore the wool of his tunic. The beast chewed wool for a moment, struggling to reach blood, and Geoffrey squeezed the hilt of his sword. The thing shook him, and Geoffrey's legs flailed, his joints creaking. The animal rose high again, towering on its hind legs, and Geoffrey saw what would destroy him.

A bear. More brown than b...
its chest. A black bone thrust...h black wax coating
arrow that had nearly killed it. From the beast, an
It fell on all fours, straddling Geof...imal was halting.
with days to contemplate what was ha...nd like a man
realized that the animal would kill hi...ing, Geoffrey
the beast was sick. ...wly because

Again, the rip of wool, a fine, clean noise, ...e a knife
into bread. The bear shook him like a long s...p of
gristle, and with a sound more than with pain, the teeth
found bone.

Geoffrey stabbed. It was difficult to stab while lying
on his back, and the sword did not slide into the beast
easily. The fur was thick on the animal's side, and Geoffrey forced the sword, his hand slippery with hot blood.
The bear deafened him with a bellow. Geoffrey
screamed, a long cry, all the words he had ever spoken,
all the words he had ever read or thought, wadded into
one throat-scalding yell, and then he rolled with a blow
that sent him like a spent top across the pine needles,
arms and legs in a tangle, until his face buried in a fern
and the beast was on him with a rattle of fury.

Geoffrey made one spasm of effort to get up, but then
it was midnight everywhere. A world pressed him into
the ground, and the air went out of him in a silent cry.

He was certain he was dead. Fern fibers squashed by
his nose made a thin keen, water squashed out of stems,
but there was no other sound. Only weight, and a shuddering. He tried to take a breath. He could not. H...
tasted humus, a black, rich flavor, the grit of it on...
teeth. He tried to cough but only groaned.

He pushed, a   n whipped across his vision. He
went nowhere   was death. The long wait for it
to end. Time   opened to the last page, when the
manuscript   and the colors are left out, and the
cover of th   ok itself exposes its underside, scarred
with impe   tions, the mottle-and-vein print of sheep-
skin.

And   en a door opened, and there was light. He
breathed, and spluttered. He was wet, and the wetness
cooled him. He struggled to his knees. He stood, sway-
ing, and an arm helped him to a place under a large
pine, where pine needles had gathered themselves in
a root crotch.

A bow fell across the brown earth, and a figure
crouched beside him. "I watched your hunting party.
I know you wish you had ferrets that would catch me."

"I have caught you." Geoffrey gripped a sleeve with
the only hand he could move. "Fortune has delivered
you to me."

"I'll stuff some dried mallow in the wounds," said
Robin Hood. "It will stop the bleeding. Don't worry.
Most of that is bear blood."

Geoffrey felt amazingly calm. Everything made sense.
The bear was a black mountain at his feet. A tick hurried
across the peak like an ebony tear, and his own hands
were clotted with red. "I've seen hunters die of less than
this," said Geoffrey. "The arm grows great and black."

"Don't be anxious."

"I'm not." Geoffrey shivered. "You've left false
    mps, haven't you? In the middle of the forest. False
    ps for my men to find."

"Yes. Will Scathlock does it well. Are your men tricked?"

"Yes."

"You would not be."

"You are safest here, at the edge of the greenwood."

"I know. To hide, do not run."

"You have saved my life," sighed the sheriff.

"The bear would have died in a moment. Your stab was near the heart. My arrow simply matched it."

"How can I kill you now that I am in your debt?"

Robin Hood laughed, delighted. "You see? A worthy man. You make it impossible for me to enjoy any triumph. You have ruined my sport. I am glad the bear did not kill you."

Geoffrey believed him. It was a painful insight: Robin Hood admired him. He hated himself, for an instant, but then put his hand to the wound in his shoulder. It began to hurt, badly. "For my part, I wish you were more like other thieves."

"More stupid?"

"More joyless."

"I hope your men continue to be clumsy."

"The falcon may miss, but it remembers the miss and next time draws blood." Geoffrey eyed Robin. The outlaw was dressed in ragged green, with gray wool stockings and tough leather shoes. The man was the color of the forest, as a lie is the color of the truth.

"Meeting you has taken the joy out of our sport," said Robin Hood. "We will soon stop playing, forever."

"If I could believe you, I would be a very happy man."

Geoffrey found his sword. The blade was smeare

with blackening syrup that a fern leaf could not wipe. Geoffrey turned back once. Robin Hood was already invisible. "I hope I never see you again," he said, not loudly but loudly enough.

He loved having the final word, but he sat down hard and felt like retching. The pain came and went, the beating of an iron heart. He stood with difficulty, and a voice behind him said, "You won't be able to make it by yourself."

Geoffrey waved the voice away and, when he found the edge of the forest, stayed there for a moment, hidden where he knew they could not see him. A ferret was held by its hind legs and gathered into a net. A brace of bloody rabbits swung from the huntsman's fist. Lady Eleanor was pink-cheeked, breathless with the pleasure of it. And beyond, the field, already bleached by the early frosts, and near the city walls, a cottage cream white in the sunlight.

This was how the world would be without him when he was gone: spread under a sky, busy with its sport, recovered from mourning and continuing. Remaining like this, half hidden, he saw the world as the angels must see it, filled with color that night would blow away, as wind erases flour spilled in the courtyard. It was all brilliant, and temporary.

They saw immediately that something was wrong. Lady Eleanor blanched and put out a hand, afraid to touch him. The huntsman tossed down the brace of rabbits. "What happened?"

"I am not as badly hurt as I seem to be. This tart 'ing on me is mostly not my blood."

"What happened?" gasped Lady Eleanor.

"My good woman, there is no need to be afraid," said Geoffrey. He took his horse's reins and then lay down, against his will—his legs folded—and he looked at the sky.

"Stand back!" commanded the huntsman, and then the man looked down at Geoffrey, as though peering into a deep hole.

Geoffrey tried to laugh

"What happened, my lord?" asked the huntsman.

"I," said Geoffrey, "have killed a bear."

THE SHERIFF'S HORSE CANTERED, eager to be within castle walls. Geoffrey tugged the rein with his good arm. Their pace slowed. Eleanor put a hand out to him to steady him in the saddle, and when the sheriff glanced her way, the look of pale concern could not be mistaken. The love of a wife is medicine, thought the sheriff.

In the courtyard Geoffrey swung himself down. Ralf had sent word of the sheriff's victory over the bear, and house servants gathered. Smiles showed on every face that met him. But something was wrong—some uneasiness troubled the house carls. Bess, Eleanor's personal servant, stood apart from the crowd.

He left the cheering throng and hurried into the castle, sending for the surgeon.

Ivo and the surgeon both hurried across the stone floor, their steps echoing. Geoffrey did not want to ask. He prayed, in nomine, like the most pious man, not the poor sinner that he was. *Let Hugh live.*

The physician clucked when he saw blood and made a hiss of compassion as he examined the wound in the light from the high windows. "But I'm afraid you've come home to troubling news, my lord," said the physician.

"Is Hugh not recovered?" asked the sheriff in a hoarse whisper.

"He has run off, my lord," said the surgeon.

"Taking a broadsword and a dagger," said Ivo.

These tidings cheered the sheriff for an instant. So Hugh was alive and quite well. But then a new concern melted his smile. What did Hugh want with a dagger, a weapon of deceit—of murder? "Where has he gone?" demanded the sheriff.

"To win honor for you, my lord," said Ivo, his eyes downcast.

Robin would not harm the sheriff's squire, Geoffrey was certain. But Robin's men might act hastily.

"Hugh is strong these recent weeks," said Ivo. "Stroke, counterstroke, lunge, and feint. And he is proud."

"But Robin Hood must be leagues away from here, my lord," said the surgeon, fumbling in his sack.

"I explained that a fox most likely keeps the town in view," said Ivo. "Leading Henry a merry chase," said the swordsman, in a tone of regret. "Hugh is a brilliant student," he added sadly.

"Robin Hood's men will cut his throat," breathed the sheriff.

35

Hugh felt the burden of his deception, deceiving the surgeon, lying. Lying sinfully, letting a shiver and a weak voice mask his actual good health. Bess slipped into his chamber and swore that she would sleep uneasy until she heard that he was well. "I prayed for your return to health," said Bess.

Hugh on his pallet of goose feathers and straw, recommended by the surgeon for its warmth and comfort, could only further his pretense by croaking, "I thank you, good Bess," in a voice like that of a very weary, very old man. Had there been a tear in Bess's eye?

But it was in the full morning, the hunting party's horses just thumping their way from the castle, that Hugh fully admitted to himself what he was doing. He felt like a shadow trailing his own body, an honest spirit watching its thieving twin, as he crept into Ivo's work-room and filched the black dagger from the wall.

A knob of bread from the surgeon's supper was all he had to break his fast, but Hugh was not hungry. Perhaps pretending illness had caused him to have a touch of symptoms, as though to feel more honest than he was. He slipped down the corridor, past the chapel, and through the tumble of gray-blue stone, masons making their chisels ring with wooden mallets, a section of outer wall under repair. No one noticed the squire hurrying past like another castle wight on an errand.

But surely a guard would glimpse him, hurrying away from the castle walls. Perhaps Bess herself, shaking out her mistress's linen from a tower window, would see him and call out.

Hugh followed the hoofprints of the hunting party easily, recalling Ivo's comment that the band of thieves would most likely eye the castle from nearby. Hugh hoped so. The thought of a long search in the forest filled him with dread.

The dagger hidden in his wool blouse, the sword heavy at his side, Hugh followed a forester's path, the trail cut years past by honorable yeomen tending the king's wood. Hugh made his way parallel to the route the cheerful hunters had taken. His plan was dim, but real enough to give him hope. If Robin Hood was near the castle, then he would hear the hunters wagering, see them, count their rabbits—and maybe lift a few from the hunters' hands before the day was done.

And if the thieves were watching, they would not be aware of a new step in the forest, someone watching them. But as the oaks closed in over Hugh, and the twitting birds made his solitude all the more perfect, he began to doubt his plan. Was it, he wondered, too late to creep back to the fastness of the castle?

How strange it was to tuck in and out of branches, listening to distant sport, conversation, laughter, the quiet of anticipation. Hugh made a wide, uneven circuit, and as he clambered over the roots of grandfather oaks, he felt the foolishness of his plan. What did Ivo know about the habits of Robin Hood?

A sword is a poor companion through nettle and dock, the shrubbery along the paths. Hugh found the crotch of an oak and sat, finishing the last crumbs from his pocket. He had seen the huntsman ask for quiet at times like this, everything already still as stone. Perhaps there was something about silence that made a hunter want more. Hugh listened. Sometimes he heard the whisper of wind in leaves and turned, expecting to see an outlaw.

But there was no one. And even the sound of the hunt was too far away, too muted by the forest, to be anything but a hint. Less than a hint—and Hugh wondered if he would be able to find his way back.

Because he would have to return, that was clear. There are no thieves to be stumbled upon by someone as guileless as myself, Hugh thought. He brushed green peat from his clothes. And stood still.

What did a bear sound like?

Much like that throaty, shattering rumble, Hugh told himself. It was too far off to be sure of the direction. Hugh ran, stumbled, splashing through a brook. His deerskin leggings were wet through. Was that another bear roar, off to the north? Hugh could not be certain. And by the time he was sure he had hurried too far, the silence was all the more perfect. His heart was beating hard and fast.

But he was lost.

A *keep*—that was what some called a castle. Because a castle kept the living whole and safe. He was as good as naked here, in the ever-twilight of the greenwood. Hugh calmed himself. He had learned from the sheriff the importance of a steady outlook. Over there, he reminded himself. The sound of a dying beast came from far over there.

But there was no path. The oak trees had not been trimmed, the youthful branches harvested, in this little-traveled copse of wasteland. A lone songbird, black as a jet brooch, squeaked, toiled upwards, and broke into song, but its tune made the silence all the more complete.

A treeful of rooks celebrated the afternoon by the time Hugh found the blood, the flattened shrubs, the snapped branches. A fly tasted the drying gouts of blood. A late-season wasp hovered over the gleaming black-red blood, and shied away.

Hugh puzzled together what had happened. A man with a sole print like the sheriff's—very like—had encountered either a bear or a bull. A bear, to judge by the tuft of black hair on a maiden-berry bush and the distinct claw marks. Hugh put his hand out to a tree to support himself. The blood was in quantities here, beyond the sweep of branches. And surely some of this blackened gore was human.

The sheriff had been hurt!

But Hugh had learned from the sheriff how to weigh evidence, how to forestall judgment, taking care, always, to trust reason. Here was the way the hunting party had followed, trailing blood from a gigantic carcass. And here was another way, a footprint pressed into the fallen leaves, and another.

Hugh almost understood what had happened, was forming a picture, his sword hand tightening round the hilt, when he heard a laugh.

A giant stepped out from behind an evergreen. Sword in hand, this huge man was a nightmare warrior, bearded, showing yellow teeth. But the giant was not looking at Hugh, even when Hugh whisked his sword from its sheath. The imposing figure looked off to one side, calm and cheerful, watching someone Hugh did not see.

"What have we, Little John?" said a voice in the shadows. Branches swayed, and Robin Hood stepped into the clearing.

36

Hugh did not speak.

"The sheriff's squire," said Robin with a smile. "Put up your weapon, Little John. This was one of my hosts when I bested the miller's son at drawing a bow. You came late to the kill," added Robin. "Your good sheriff survived a bear, no less."

"He's not hurt?" Hugh heard himself ask.

"A nip, a little wound," said Robin.

Relief weakened Hugh for an instant, and then he recalled his purpose. "I have come to win honor for the sheriff," said Hugh.

Amusement was bright in Robin's eyes. "Honor!" He laughed. "A good thing, although not as fine as a warm fire on a wet night."

"The sheriff has been merciful," said Hugh. "Patient, charitable—and brave."

"Your sheriff is an honorable man—"

Hugh angled his sword upwards in an unmistakable gesture. "I call upon you to match blades with me, Robin Hood," he said, uttering a challenge, just as the knights in songs were known to do, although Hugh had never heard it done himself.

Robin put his hands on his hips, and Hugh realized that the outlaw was armed only with a longbow, slung over his back. "A challenge would have to be weighed seriously, squire," said Robin Hood.

"I challenge you before God," said Hugh, marveling at his own pluck, his bravado, his near-mad courage. "Before Saint Michael, Our Lady—" Hugh stopped himself. To swear by such holy names was close to sinfulness, unless a man was in dead earnest.

"Strong speech," said Robin, almost sadly. The outlaw crooked the fingers on one gloved hand, and a figure in Lincoln green stepped to his side, carrying a sword and belt. Quickly the bow was whipped from his shoulder and handed over to his man, and Robin Hood fastened the sword onto his hip. As he worked the buckle, the outlaw said, "You are not born of the castle, I think."

"My father was Peter, an armorer." Honesty prompted Hugh to name a slightly more lowly, and more actual, craft for his parent. "A good Christian greaver. My name is Hugh, and I am one of the sheriff's men."

"The man of his right hand, I would guess. Craftier than the lot of them," said Robin. "A few of my band led Henry and his cohorts off and off, into the north."

He smiled. "If your honor demands swordplay, we'll sport awhile. Although the truth is I am in no fighting spirit myself."

His gently mocking tone was embellished with some warm feeling Hugh could barely guess. It was kindness, Hugh decided as he took a fighting stance. Kindness, and something like a patronizing tone. Hugh felt anger—cold, fighting anger. He took a quick step and made a false lunge, what Ivo called a Frenchman's stab, all feint and little power. It was what a swordsman did when he wanted to deceive his opponent into thinking how easy this game would be.

But even such a decorative attack drew Robin's sword from its sheath. The blue light of the afternoon sky and the black claws of overhead branches reflected off the steel. Robin Hood made a salute with his blade, teased his steel out to touch Hugh's, and then stepped easily, sword balanced in his hand, not a swordsman so much as a man at play.

Hugh had often wondered if he had the power in his heart to kill a man. The power, and the malice. Hugh begged the forgiveness of Heaven, and while Robin Hood tested his footing, toeing aside the dry, yellow leaves underfoot, Hugh double-stepped and skewered the outlaw.

Except that at the last instant Robin Hood danced and was behind Hugh, tickling the sleeve of Hugh's blouse with the point of his weapon. Hugh parried, the ring of steel on steel shocking, real. This was not courtyard play. This was not Ivo hacking at half speed with a sword fettled in the castle. This was a man wanted by the law, fighting off Hugh's blow with a sword that rang sweetly. Spanish metal, thought Hugh, or something even finer, Damascus steel.

And from the moment Robin Hood began to drive Hugh back, with a kindly light in his eyes, still at play, it was clear. For all my practice, thought Hugh, Robin Hood will kill me easily.

Footwork, Hugh reminded himself. Footwork and surprise. The two of them parried, swung, counterstroked, like two opponents hoping to make as much noise as possible, the ringing steel a bright, astounding music in the quiet forest. Fluid as his movements were, the outlaw was quicker. And stronger. Hugh's wrist and arm were already tired. Little John chuckled as Robin worked easily, defending himself from a furious attack that had Hugh sweating and Robin barely breathing hard.

The sword was too heavy! Robin Hood's sword must be growing heavy, too, but the outlaw switched hands, altering his stance, and fought as cunningly left-handed as before. A fierce stitch in his side had Hugh bending sideways, and his vision was growing vague. The sound, like woodsmen dragging branches, step by step, was his own breath, hot in his throat.

For a long time, for an age, Hugh kept Robin Hood off, blocking, parrying, lunging, but the young man fought at the limit of his power, while Robin Hood had an easy smile, uttering encouragement: "Good stroke! Again—a real arm on this squire, Little John!"

Bitter, even desperate, Hugh blinked as sweat stung his eyes. The iron ringing music of the swords vibrated up his arm, into his shoulder. His body ached.

"And he's fast on his feet," said Robin Hood. "You could learn from him, John."

At the last, his legs growing weak, Hugh stepped back, feinted, feinted again, mock lunges intended to break his opponent's rhythm. Hugh drove his sword towards the outlaw's breast, carrying the point on a straight line, guiding it true, footwork exact, sword arm locked at the elbow, left arm held as a counterbalance. But Robin stepped sideways and closed, embracing Hugh, laughing.

"I've been taught a lesson today, Little John," said Robin, panting.

Hugh sank to his knees, breathing too hard to speak.

"I've been taught a lesson in blade style and courage," said Robin Hood gently. He knelt beside Hugh on one knee. "You have defended the sheriff's honor well. He would be proud."

Hugh's hand crept into his blouse. All the while, during the fight, Hugh had been aware of this other, secret blade. His fist closed over the hilt. Perhaps this dagger had been an extra weight, a distraction. Maybe the presence of this heavy knife had cost him victory. But, Hugh thought, I carried it here for a reason.

This was still the moment, before the outlaw knew what was happening. The hilt of the dagger was warm, and Hugh saw how easy it would be. How many times had he seen a roebuck cut, throat opened, body drained of blood? Here was Robin Hood, bright-eyed, unaware. A quick move, one quick stab, and it would be over. Something in Robin Hood's eyes told Hugh that the outlaw knew, he knew there was a dagger, a stiletto, some night knife secreted in Hugh's blouse.

Now was the time.

The moment was passing. They both rose to their feet. Robin folded his arms, regarding Hugh.

With a long, chilling whisper, the giant drew a sword from a blackened, worn scabbard at his side. Robin glanced, and the giant stayed where he was.

"And you continue to win honor," said Robin Hood, in a voice quite different now, neither amused nor kind. "By knowing when to strike and when to stay your hand."

Hugh did not know how he knew the manner—what rhyme he had heard, what minstrel tale, had taught him how to act. Hugh bowed, briefly—like a man of court, a gentleman, a knight. On any other day before this he would have blushed, feeling false.

"Little John, I pray you accompany Hugh, the sheriff's man, to the castle," said Robin Hood, adopting the high speech a man would use in the company of a man-at-arms. "If not to the walls, certainly within sight of them."

"I thank you, sir," said Hugh, in a voice he could barely recognize as his own. "And trust we may meet again."

How can I speak like this? wondered Hugh.

"The hope is welcome to my heart," said Robin.

Hugh turned back at the edge of the clearing, and Robin gazed after him. But when Hugh looked back again, the man was gone.

37

Geoffrey was surprised how happy he was to see Hugh.

They sat in the dining hall. Hugh's leggings were muddy, but otherwise he looked no worse for his brief stay in the forest. The sheriff sent for Ivo, and Hugh returned the dagger to the swordsman with a stammered apology,

"I'll feel all the better if you give me your word this went unused," said Ivo.

"I could not bring myself to cut a throat," said Hugh, his eyes downcast.

"And I thank Heaven for that, Hugh," said Ivo.

"Why does he teach weaponry and then fear the thought of a cut throat?" asked Hugh when Ivo was gone.

Geoffrey listened to Hugh's story. Sword to sword

with the outlaw: it was an exciting tale, and the sheriff knew it was true. The young man was different now, chastened, pale. And there was some other quality the sheriff could not name. Hugh ate a chunk of loaf bread hungrily, and a wedge of cheese, washing it all down with small beer.

"I am sorry I deceived you," said Hugh. "I wanted—"

Geoffrey raised a finger.

"Let me tell you all that happened when I was the guest of Robin Hood," said the sheriff.

"No need," said Hugh, not eager for the sheriff to embarrass himself. "The kitchen is full of the story of it—"

Geoffrey put his elbows on the oak table, the overcloth and tablecloth both taken away earlier in the day to be shaken and aired in the sun. The sheriff told his story. He recalled every word, every detail.

When he was done, the two sat quietly, house stewards clearing away the dishes, wiping the crumbs.

"Do you hate the man?" asked Hugh at last.

"Robin Hood? Hate him?" Geoffrey wanted to say that of course, he hated any enemy of the king. But instead he laughed quietly, almost silently, and said, "Come with me, Hugh. Today we have another sort of outlaw to contend with."

A PEASANT GIRL USED a besom to sweep the street in front of her doorway, a bundle of broom that was too big for her. She stopped to watch the two riders pass. A white kerchief sheltered her head, and her white apron flowed nearly to the ground.

As they approached the mill, a crabbed figure stole from the doorway and stood in the road. "My lord," said the stooped figure, "my bear wore itself out on me so it was too weak for you."

"It was not weak, exactly," said Geoffrey.

"No healthy bear can maul a man and he walk away, my lord. Although we all grant it was a fine and brave thing to stick it to death."

Geoffrey pulled at the rein, and by accident his punctured shoulder bunched. He nearly gasped but instead looked away and screwed his features up, as if studying the weather.

"A fine thing to slay a bear, be it sick, drunk, or otherwise," continued the miller, "and my son might be given a bit of credit, too, for filling him with enough arrows to make him weak."

Geoffrey listened hard for a hint that he might not have killed the bear without help, but there was only the gaping mouth of the miller waiting for a compliment regarding his son. Geoffrey was glad to give it. The miller did not bother to hide his stiffness, while Geoffrey tried to disguise the pain his shoulder gave him, and every other part of his body, too, whenever he moved. "He's a fine archer, a sure hand, and a steady eye."

"Nearly the match of Robin Hood, they tell me."

Geoffrey studied the miller as he spoke, but there was no telltale gleam. "It may well be, although how could we ever know?"

"Some say there's a way of knowing. That Robin Hood paid my lord sheriff a visit and that there was an archery match between my son and Robin, before your eyes. Although, at the time, you did not know it."

Geoffrey leaned forwards, and grinned with pain. "This is true. Robin Hood came in a disguise. As a potter, good miller. A counterfeit potter, and we were deceived."

Geoffrey had expected the truth to disarm the miller, but the miller limped forwards and clutched the bridle of Geoffrey's horse. "In your own castle, before your wife and servants, my lord?"

"Indeed."

"Then the rest is true. How he led you into the greenwood?" The miller paused, and then, when Geoffrey said nothing, continued. "And there held a feast, a mocking feast?"

Geoffrey made a quiet laugh. A false laugh, at first, a way of hiding his anger, but in a moment it was genuine. "Yes, all true. But miller, you should know something."

"And what is that, my lord?"

"Robin Hood is a much better archer than your son."

"WE HAVE COME about the pigs," said Geoffrey.

The abbess looked away, at the window, as if she could see through the translucent glass. "I know why you are here. I would not bother to see you, except that this time, Lord Sheriff, I want you to be sure this will never happen again."

"That is my wish entirely."

The presence of Hugh obviously disappointed her, because she forced a pleasant smile and gestured round her. "Do you like our library?"

Geoffrey did not glance to either side. He stared straight at the abbess, one half of her face illuminated by light from the window. "I wish I had time to examine it more carefully. Unfortunately . . ."

"Certainly you have a moment to look at this." She opened what was apparently the finest volume of all, so special it had a stand of its own, like a lectern a priest might use, but here there would never be any homily, and no worshipers.

"Some other time, perhaps," said Geoffrey.

"We should never be in too great a hurry for spiritual nourishment."

Geoffrey bowed and stepped to the book. An angel knelt before Mary, flourishing a scroll that read, "*Ave gratia plena.*" The Annunciation. The white dove descended to Mary, and Mary looked up from the Scriptures she was studying. The angel's wings poised behind him. He was changing human history, but even so, he would stay only a few moments. Both the angel and Mary wore halos, their holiness delivered on golden plates. The halos caught the light and gave it back into the room in the soft, steady gleam of real gold. This one page was more valuable than his father's entire library.

"Thank you for showing me this," said Geoffrey. "It makes everything so clear."

"Is it not one of the most beautiful things you have ever seen?"

"Perhaps the most beautiful."

"Ah, you flatter me. But we are proud of it."

"The pigs, Lady Emily."

She allowed a dimple to appear and vanish in her cheek. Geoffrey was pleased: she was annoyed. "I wanted you to see perfect beauty, before you looked upon beauty savaged." They followed in her wake. "I don't know why these beasts behave as they do," she said.

"This time of year the peasants feed their herds by letting them graze on acorns, and I think they become too happy to be free and eating."

She turned, wrinkling her nose. She was not surprised that Geoffrey had a sympathy with swine. "Our Lord put a gang of devils into such a herd, and they rushed over a cliff."

"Alas, Lady Emily, we have no cliffs." Implying that they did have devils.

"There!" she said, holding forth her arm dramatically, a pageant Pilate calling, "Behold the Man!"

Pig sign was everywhere, even to the squashed black of pig dung. Small white flowers Geoffrey did not recognize, bunches of white, had been torn like a blanket to get at the earth.

"Alyssum," she said.

"They must have been beautiful."

"They were."

"And will be, I hope, once again."

She showed Geoffrey her profile. "If God wills it."

The echo of the Crusaders' cry, "God wills it!," may have been intended to demonstrate Geoffrey's own lack of vigor, but instead it made the abbess seem deliberately helpless. "They came through the hedge," said Geoffrey.

"Just as before."

"They no doubt left this place and hid in the King's Forest."

"That is exactly where they went, although I have no idea where they are now."

"Of course not. How can a good woman like yourself be expected to note the travels of pigs?"

Outside the abbey walls Geoffrey was content to walk his horse. He felt that he should explain the abbess to Hugh, but could not begin. "A person like the abbess," Geoffrey said. "A woman like the abbess—" he broke off. Continuing to think of her as a woman was a mistake. "Finds beauty the most important thing in the world. It reminds her, I think, of Heaven."

"She is very proud," offered Hugh.

"Yes, although her pride is not such a great disfigurement. Although," he hastened to add, "still, no doubt, at least a small sin."

The hills were the color of breath on a silver plate. Fields that had been green only days ago were suddenly acorn brown. A peasant walked away from a pile of branches and gathered another branch, a scribble of black lightning he placed upon the pile. Everything was gathered in. The land was slow, like the steady breath of a sleeper. The road was more prominent now than at any other time of year, the step-impacted earth bright, like a long, straight tear across brown cloth.

In the distance a herd of pigs gathered under a stand

of oaks. A peasant lifted a staff and struck a tree, and acorns showered, invisible at this distance. The pigs squirmed together where the nuts fell, and the peasant stopped working and looked across the field to Geoffrey. The man wiped his forehead with his sleeve and continued to work. A dog looked on, grinning as dogs do when they are satisfied, and Geoffrey wondered how many times he had seen such a sight, peasants working without speech in a world of animals, nearly animals themselves.

Geoffrey rode hard, and pigs scattered, grunting. Their bunched tails and flat, mobile snouts seemed suddenly like the perfect disguise for a devil.

The peasant wore a black cap and a pig-colored tunic. A bramble clung to his tattered stockings, a miniature ox-horn. He wished the sheriff good day, and Geoffrey made a show of having to restrain a spirited horse from riding further into the herd. "Pigman," said Geoffrey.

"My lord?"

"Do not trespass on the abbey grounds or I will slaughter your swine." He spoke slowly, clearly. The peasant bowed, and Geoffrey was nearly certain this was not the right herd. How difficult it was to be right about anything.

Hugh galloped from the edge of the forest wild-eyed. His horse was dark with sweat, and Hugh wept where a branch had lashed him. "My lord!" he managed.

"What's wrong? What is it?"

"I have found something amazing!"

"What is it?"

"Something the pigs dug up!"

"What?"

"Come see—I can't tell you."

"I will go nowhere unless you tell me what it is."

"It is—a treasure!"

38

They stood in the forest, the smell of tree decay all round them. The mulch had been torn by pigs rooting for acorns, and the roots of the oak were exposed here and there, wooden worms tangled and snapped. Two leather skulls gathered to a topknot fastened with blackened cord. One of the cords had been loosened.

"Look!" breathed Hugh.

Geoffrey was afraid to touch it for a moment. He took the heavy sack with trembling fingers. He peered into the wet leather and saw only darkness. He stepped into a puddle of light, and a crowd of small suns smiled up at him. The slick leather slipped from his fingers, and they both gasped.

But it did not spill. A single yellow moon slid across a root and floated there on the surface of the black earth. Hugh picked it up and held it between his fingers.

"Is it," Hugh asked hoarsely, "real?"

"Is it real!" But doubt is easily shared, and Geoffrey took the yellow disc into his own fingers. He opened his hand. The coin slipped into the very center of his palm, the midpoint, instantly warm with his touch.

He closed his hand round it. "It's real," he said. "You have found the thief's treasure. Our poor thief! Still rotting on the gibbet."

"The pigs found it," Hugh said. "I simply stumbled over it."

"What do you think we mean by 'finding' something? We stumble on nearly everything that happens to us— and we have to know a treasure when we fall on it. You have a good eye, Hugh. A good, alert eye, like a merlin."

THEIR HORSES WERE blotchy with sweat by the time they returned to the castle. Geoffrey knew that some of the thief's victims would come forward to claim their due. But he also knew that the king's purse would be fatter in a day or two, and he planned the report he would write. He would, of course, ignore the swine. But he would praise Hugh, in a way that reflected Geoffrey's shrewd ability to appoint helpers.

"Sir Roger!" cried Geoffrey. "You are looking well!"

The old man sat in the sunlight of the courtyard, a sword across his knee and a staff in his hand. His white hair lifted in a gust of wind. "Well enough to soak up sun," said Sir Roger.

Geoffrey told him about the trove Hugh had discovered, and the old Crusader smiled. "A good eye and perhaps the help of Heaven," he said. "You are fortunate in each other."

LADY ELEANOR TOOK the dog off her lap. "Shouldn't you lie down?"

It was evening, and Geoffrey felt empty of color, like the hills around the city, and the fields beside the roads. At last he uncorked the poppy wine and sipped.

Lady Eleanor made pleasant conversation for a while, the sort of talk that softened a room, like a tapestry, and then she stopped herself and put a finger on Geoffrey's lips, even though he had been saying nothing.

Geoffrey realized that he had been beguiled into her chamber. Not tricked so much as led like a horse. It was darker out than he had realized, and there was the honey scent of beeswax from the candles round them. "I'm worried about you," she was saying.

"No, you aren't."

"No, I'm not. You can take care of yourself. But what I mean to say is—I want you to lie with me. And yet I feel that you are too injured."

Geoffrey sipped the wine. A taste like resin, but darker, numbed his tongue. "Too damaged for love?"

HE HAD FORGOTTEN how well he knew his wife's body and what pleasure it could give. So pale, in the light of

one candle, and then, no candles at all, darkness—
and her body with its own light, a messenger not from
Heaven but from the world of the daughters of men.
She was as warm as just-quickened wax, and she spoke
his name in his ear like a secret, a magic name only the
two of them knew.

He woke much later, suddenly, like a small door
springing open. She was beside him in the bed, and the
canopy had been pulled round them. There was only
silence and the sound of her breathing. He was like a
field after rain, changed entirely, if only because it lay
under a clean sky.

39

The Fool was standing on his head, pointing his feet towards the ceiling and wiggling them. Hugh trailed behind the sheriff, and for a moment Geoffrey could read his squire's thoughts. "Go ahead, try it," said the sheriff. "Add to your many talents."

Hugh laughed and followed Geoffrey into the room.

"I'm sorry I'm late, good surgeon. A lad stole a flitch of bacon from the market, and I had the good luck to be in the market at the time. Or bad luck, actually, since I am not overfond of dragging peasant boys into the prison."

"You look very fit, my lord, for a man just mauled by a bear."

"It hurts very badly, good surgeon. No, don't touch it. Please. Well, if you must."

"No swelling." The surgeon lifted the dressing suspiciously. "No poisons." He frowned, thoughtful and, it seemed, nearly disappointed. "You say you stuffed the wounds with mallow?"

"That's right."

"Dried mallow."

"Exactly."

"I've never heard of such a cure."

"Oh, I wouldn't say it was a cure. Just a sop for the blood until the real cure takes place. Under good hands like yours."

"It seems to have worked. I would rather have you eat a theriac prepared with the blood of bear, but without another bear at hand . . ."

"They are scarce."

"Yes," sniffed the surgeon.

"You seem unhappy, my friend."

They were both surprised at this. The surgeon was, as Geoffrey knew, friend to very few. The surgeon looked away, patting himself with both hands. "I am so forgetful these days."

"So many things concern you."

"Yes. The brain is like a treasure chest: when it is full, something must be removed in order to add something."

"It's not so bad to be forgetful. You may forget unpleasant things."

"My apprentice has run away."

Geoffrey paused in adjusting his tunic. "Run away?"

The surgeon put a hand to his cap, and then walked to the window, shaking. "I'm sorry, good sheriff. It was last night. It happens. An apprentice can't manage his duties. He suffers a change of heart. Oh, it's difficult, the work we have to do. But I saw a great future in him."

"I'm sorry."

"A great future." The surgeon turned. His eyes were red, and he gathered his basket with hands that fumbled, spilling a leather sack of herbs. "Oh, my myrtle. It darkens the hair, as you know. Used with crocus, of course. I told you this."

"Did you? I can't remember."

"Neither can I. We have a great deal on our minds, you and I."

"Yes. And if you will forgive my saying so, we are both condemned to fail much of the time."

The surgeon looked down at his basket, tucking in the last of his myrtle. "I don't know, my lord . . ."

"People die. Outlaws escape."

"And apprentices run away. His knowledge will make him wealthy. He can claim to know how to cure the wens, the sprains, the falling sickness, all of it. He can claim stolen knowledge, and people will gather round him, because he will be cheaper than a surgeon."

"I will tell everyone that your dressings drew the poison from my wounds."

"Do you know that in the Holy Land there is a snake that spits poison? You pass it, and it fires venom through the air. Now, how is an apprentice going to cure people in a world so foul, so fallen that the creature damned by God Himself spits fatal darts?"

"He will find it very difficult."

"He will find it impossible. In summer the very air is

235

a pestilence. The gases above a marsh can raise a pustule with just a twitch of the wind. How can an apprentice cure in a world so treacherous? He will find it totally impossible. He has the Latin of a traveling player, the French of a tavern slut, and the manners of—why, the dogs at your table, my lord, the graceful whippets, are better-mannered than that once-mewed finch. I was a great fool to suffer his impatience, for even a moment. When he didn't accept his duty of reading to Sir Roger with good cheer, I should have beaten him to a paste, and that's God's truth."

"Good surgeon, there will be other apprentices—"

"Damn that ungrateful badger pig. Smug and proud, thinking himself the perfect little surgeon. Forgive me, my lord, but I feel the spleen running through the vents of my body like spring rain. Oh, how strong it makes me feel to have this fury—this fury of the justly enraged—in my blood. Therefore—" The surgeon paused at the door, like a man at the edge of a cliff over which he was about to fly. "Therefore, I leave you now to rearrange my plans and find a new apprentice, one who knows his duty like a dog."

There was a clatter of horses, a great choir of snorting and clopping, and cries of "Here!" and "Ho!"

"It sounds," said Geoffrey, "as though an army has ridden into the courtyard."

A FIGURE STUMBLED into the chamber. It was glistening with sweat, and forest mud starred its leather breastplate. "My lord!" it gasped.

"Henry?"

"I bring you a prize."

"What sort of prize, good Henry?"

"A prize stolen from Robin Hood!"

Geoffrey went cold and felt for a bedpost, simply to have something solid in his grasp. When he could speak, he said, "What have you stolen?"

"One of his men!"

Geoffrey felt a small wave of relief but stiffened at once. "How did you manage—"

"Days and nights, my lord, we hounded them. Still-warm ashes, and game hanging from trees, and the stink of them. The smell of that band forever shut off from human comfort."

Geoffrey splashed wine into a goblet. "Here, Henry, please. It will steady you."

Henry slurped. "Thank you, my lord. It tastes better than anything in the world after nothing but moss water."

Geoffrey made a gesture of welcome and of impatience.

"Camp after camp we followed them, always minutes behind. They must have been terrified of us, so deep in the forest, the sheriff's men, the dogs of the king, breathing hot on their napes!"

"I have no doubt. Please, continue."

Henry wiped his lips with his fist. "Finally I sent the forester ahead and kept the rest of the men back, cutting wood and sneezing, making all the noise a band of hearty men could make. And this good man saw a figure, sprinting like a deer through the trees, and followed him on a parallel path through the forest. Robin Hood has his sly ways, but we have ours. Our good forester crept like a weasel and watched while this outlaw lay down under a tree; the forester stepped forth as easy as a man stepping up to table, I have no doubt, and pressed his good steel against the criminal's throat!"

"Who is it, then?"

"And then he dragged the wretch back to the rest of us, and we had by that time crept forwards ourselves, sly as stoats, if you'd only seen us! And when that felon looked upon the good men who had him, he fell to his knees for his soul."

"Who is it?"

"I'll bring him in to you now, my lord, and you can see him for yourself. A miserable beast he is, I must say, befouled and besmeared, and a shameful thing to drag into your good presence."

Success had made Henry eloquent. Geoffrey watched out the window, but he could see only a mill of sweaty horses and dismounted men, talking quietly in the usual after-hunt manner.

The door burst wide, and a heap of green rags was thrown to the stone floor.

40

There he is, Lord Sheriff!" said Henry. "One of those filthy whelps who kept you prisoner!"

The heap stirred, and a head lifted and looked at Geoffrey. The man made a small smile of recognition, even of friendship. And of regret. Regret that his life was now forfeit, that a slow death at the hands of an expert was all the future he had.

Geoffrey walked to the trembling figure and knelt. He looked hard into the face of Will Scathlock. Will looked down and sighed. This was the end of his life. Like most men, he understood that he could not escape forever, but he had hoped to die much later, and in some pleasant place far from his enemies. His posture, even the wet prints his hands left on the stones, spoke of fear and also of acceptance.

Geoffrey stood and walked to the window. He controlled almost nothing in his life. His life controlled him. He was a spider fastened to his web. He had no more freedom than a peg driven into the leg of a chair. He was locked deep, and mallet-flattened, and all he could do was breathe and love or hate his life.

The horses were fewer, and the courtyard reflected sunlight. The blacksmith had begun to work again, and the clank of his hammer touched Geoffrey, a bell, miscast and unmusical, ringing across a far greater space than a courtyard.

He turned. "This is not one of Robin Hood's men."

Henry's mouth fell open.

"I have never seen this man before."

"But he was in the forest. He was running. He—" Henry opened a hand. He could not speak. "We found him."

"You did find him, good Henry, and you have done very well. But this is not one of the band."

"Perhaps he was a part of the band who was out hunting when you—"

"No, Henry. I think not. This is an innocent man."

"Innocent!"

"What crime has he committed?"

Henry made a huge shrug.

"Although I grant you that no Christian spends his days in the forest. He meant some sort of minor harm. Poaching. Gathering the king's wood. Oh, I recognize this sort of man. Little better than a sheep tick. But we can scarcely rack him because he is worthless."

Will looked up without a sign of complicity.

"I want never to see you again," said Geoffrey, partly

for effect, but partly in truth. "I want you to go far from here and never return. If you have companions, tell them this: I have returned your life, and I expect peace."

"I thank you, gracious lordship," said the toothless mouth.

"Leave me," said Geoffrey, waving as at a fly.

Henry stepped forwards to haul the man away but stopped as the man stood and slipped to the door. Will looked back with one last glance of gratitude and also of promise.

"A wretch," said Geoffrey.

"Yes," said Henry in a dismal voice. "A great wretch."

"Comfort yourself, Henry." Geoffrey gripped him by the shoulders. "You have done well, and I am proud of you."

"Yes?"

"Indeed. Prepare yourself for a feast."

"But we have to set out again. Robin Hood is still out there, waiting."

"Let him wait. Let him wait forever. He will mean nothing to us. We have better things to do than chasing shadows in the greenwood."

"Yes," said Henry, bewildered. "Better things."

"Be happy, Henry! We've won."

Henry nodded, a man pretending to understand.

41

Geese flapped their wings, sending white feathers into the bright sunlight. Two white-aproned egg sellers tried to outbid each other. New ale was sampled at one end of the market, where the men gathered. "By my faith this is good," said a franklin, in his best market day tunic and belt. He gave Hugh and Bess a friendly nod as they passed.

The folk were pink-cheeked, baskets of apples and pitchers of cider from the south giving cheer to the clear, cold afternoon. A few of the sheriff's men, in their newly polished leather, joined in the swapping of tales beside a pie seller, squab pies the specialty. Bess was on Hugh's arm, and even though dray horses exhaled white vapor, Hugh did not feel cold. A pullet in a cage pecked at a boy's out-thrust fingers, and a dog wagged its tail, hoping for a scrap.

Ivo met Hugh's eye, the old swordsman sampling cheese from a huge wedge, nodding in agreement: excellent, and no doubt worth the price. But his attention was on Hugh, who walked with his new sword on one hip. The weapon did not feel strange. A gift from Ivo, it hung as if it belonged where it was. Ivo smiled.

Only one ugly sound marred the marketplace.

A voice was uttering indistinct words that Hugh began to understand only when he stopped and listened. "Let's go look at those baskets," Bess said.

"Our bootmaker's son, spending an idle moment with the ladies," Thurstin was saying.

"Pay him no attention," whispered Bess.

Hugh walked a few steps, avoiding a splash of goose dirt, but he found himself turning, unable to ignore what Thurstin was saying.

"Good hound Hugh, the sheriff's brachet cur," called Thurstin. Thurstin had a few companions, red-faced, broad-shouldered men, but the market swirled and parted round these individuals.

"He's a clever sheriff's man, but not so sly he can catch himself a purse fox," said Thurstin. "Not so smart he can catch Robin Hood!"

Few joined in the laughter. Something about the sheriff's dignity and Hugh's new sword communicated itself to the people of the town. The townfolk felt protective towards the sheriff and Hugh, loyal to them. The two had failed to capture the famous outlaw, but the general belief was that Robin's continuing freedom was because of the outlaw's great good luck and did not reflect on the earnestness or courage of the sheriff or Hugh.

Hugh drew close to Thurstin. "The king's law is against riot and unlawful demeanor," said Hugh quietly.

"Listen to this whelp mouth the law," said Thurstin.

But now even the most unsteady of Thurstin's companions had backed off, leaving him alone.

"Let's see you silence me, squire," said Thurstin.

Hugh said nothing.

"Let's see you put a fist in my mouth," bawled Thurstin, spit spray and ale breath making Hugh step back.

"Let your friends take you home, Thurstin," said Hugh.

Thurstin's companions closed in on their friend, leading him away. Thurstin struggled clumsily, but he made no progress against their collective strength.

"Do you know him?" asked Bess as they passed a table piled with baskets woven from yellow reeds.

Hugh could think of many things to say, because certainly even Bess knew of Thurstin. He's no one of any importance, he thought of saying. Or, in a flare of honesty, he might have said, He used to bully me. Instead he said, "He's not so ill-tempered when he's taken less ale. He draws a bow with a steady hand."

"But not as steady as Robin Hood," said Bess, leaning in to Hugh, her head against him. She smelled of rare spices, the stuff of legends, perfumes Hugh barely knew, cinnamon, nutmeg.

THE DOVES GATHERED in the dovecot, gray and white birds tucking themselves into the half-moon–shaped openings. It was late afternoon, and Geoffrey walked through shadows as cold as pond water, and when sunlight broke over his shoulders, it was barely warm.

The chapel held its own warmth. The stone arches seemed radiant with it. The Mother of God waited in the perfect silence, a figure carved out of silence itself, as if there were quarries of the stuff in distant mountains.

"You see, my lord," whispered the glassmaker. "You can't tell it was ever missing."

The blue sections of sky above the angels were intact. The angels posed with their trumpets and staffs, their halos expanding round their heads, and the perfect blue was over all of them, the afternoon sun staining it a deeper shade, as if even in Heaven days grew short in the seasons of eternity.

"It was a simple matter," said the glassmaker. The new leading was seamless, the black border between sections not only of sky, but the angels themselves, the entire window fitted together with a complex of black veins, a net that dragged the air and caught color.

"You have made it beautiful again," breathed the sheriff.

The glassmaker bowed.

This glasswork had not been simple. It had taken care and the experience of years. It was all man-made, this glass, the statue, the dying Christ, the chapel itself, all the work of human patience. Even the image of Saint Peter in the corner, treading the shadowy ground. He carried the key to Heaven. The key was large, and it was heavy. More than anything, Peter seemed to want to put the key down, but he could not, as if the powers of Heaven were as bound as the powers of earth.

Geoffrey strode across the courtyard. The Fool walked on his hands to a place the sheriff could not avoid without altering his path. Geoffrey paused and gave the Fool's ankles a squeeze.

Then the sheriff hurried into the castle beneath a sound like hands clapping, steadily, calmly, the wings of another dove home before dark.

Michael Cadnum is the acclaimed author of more than a dozen novels, including *Taking It*, *Edge*, and *Zero at the Bone* (all available in Puffin editions). His work has been twice nominated for the Mystery Writers of America's Edgar Allan Poe Award. Michael Cadnum lives in Albany, California.